Twice Upon a Time There Lived

Robert Philip Bolton

Also by Robert Philip Bolton
The Artist as an Old Man (Self Portrait)
It's What Eddie Did
The Fable of Flitcroft Point
Jacko. One Bloke. One Year.
The Boys and Men of Auckland's Mickey Rooney Gang
The Fine Art of Kindness
Six Murders?
To The White Gate
Underneath The Arclight
My Marian Year
The Boltons of The Little Boltons
The Tapu Garden of Eden
For Viktor. The story of Mussorgsky's 'Pictures at an Exhibition'
The Collected Short Stories
(in which is combined *Nana's Special Day and other stories*, *The Dolphin and other stories*, and *Quickies*.)

Robert Philip Bolton was born in New Zealand in 1945. He has been writing fiction most of his adult life. Most of his work is about New Zealand and New Zealanders. He lives in Auckland.

Twice Upon a Time
There Lived

Robert Philip Bolton

Prologue

If, for some reason, you are strolling aimlessly south along Mount Eden Road in Auckland one summer evening — although why you would is uncertain — you might notice a wooden post almost hidden in a boundary hedge on the corner of Brockley Street. There, if you part the straggling and untamed hedge, you will find a large wooden arrow, pointing up the street, into which is neatly carved and painted the legend THE BROCKLEY MANSION. Nothing else. And then, if overtaken by curiosity, and with nothing else to do, you turn off Mount Eden Road to continue your stroll up the gentle slope of Brockley Street, you will be struck by an imposing two-storied wooden Victorian mansion standing on the lower slopes of Maungawhau, whose great volcanic bulk looms behind it, looking imperiously down the hill, seeming to dominate the entire neighbourhood.

When at last you reach the top of the street you'll find, at that late hour, that the tall double wrought-iron gates, set into the old scoria walls but in a modern style, are closed and locked. Beyond the gates you will see a broad drive, a mere continuation of the street, which, for the entire hundred and forty years the house was a home, was neither sealed nor gated. The drive sweeps up to the mansion's front veranda where it circles into a convenient return as well as continuing, to the right of the house and then behind it, out of sight, to the original stables.

Through the gates, to the left, close to the stone wall and capped by its own sheltering awning, is a large sign, professionally painted but somewhat faded by Auckland's sun and rain:

WELCOME TO BROCKLEY HOUSE
Open to the public daily 9.00 am — 4.30 pm
Free Admission

This grand Victorian mansion was built in 1872 by Ebenezer Partington Brockley, a merchant of this city, who once farmed the land now occupied by the houses in Brockley Street and adjacent Charlotte and Ebenezer Streets, as well as the 1.2 hectares of land on which the house stands which was bought from the Māori owners in 1868. The architect of the house is not recorded but is thought to have been Sir Lancelot Haxondale, a personal friend of Mr Brockley. However, the interior furnishings and fittings were personally chosen by Mr Brockley and imported by him from his home city of Manchester, England. Following his death in 1914 his descendants, as if under instruction, made no changes to the building's exterior and, with the exception of installing electric lighting and cooking in 1934, and the telephone in 1951, made only minor changes to the interior. As a result, the house's perfectly maintained furniture, fittings, carpets, appliances and lighting remain as they were when it and its land were bequeathed to the citizens of Auckland, "for their enjoyment and education", by the recluse owner, Mr William Conwyne, Ebenezer Brockley's great-grandson, when he died in 2011. A considerable sum of money was also left in trust to provide for the maintenance of the house and its grounds which are managed and maintained by the Parks Department of the City of Auckland.

PART ONE

Chapter 1

Early one wintry morning in the year of Our Lord — a phrase rarely heard now but in common use then — nineteen thirty-six, in a private nursing home in Mount Eden, near the Crystal Palace picture house where the worried young man in the waiting room worked as a projectionist, a lovely young woman, his wife, was effortlessly giving birth to the couple's first and, as it turned out, only child: a strong and healthy baby girl.

Having quickly slipped free from the confines of her mother's belly, writhing and wriggling and stretching as if celebrating her freedom, she — the slimy and somewhat bloody infant — squealed and screamed in response to her first breath of the delivery room's chilly air and the stern accoucheuse's sharp smack on her tiny, pointed, red and wrinkled bottom.

At that time in our history the father — any father — was not permitted to attend the delivery room to see his baby being born or even to support and comfort his wife. No professional thought was given to the emotional stress being suffered in unknowing isolation by the husband and father.

But so quiet, early and dark was that long-ago winter morning — the newborn child would be three hours into her life before her unripe eyes would sense daylight — that the anxious father, chain smoking in the dimly lighted and unwarmed waiting room, down a long, uncarpeted and echoing corridor, easily heard the thin cries of what he knew must be his own child.

Stubbing out his cigarette in a full ashtray, and immediately lighting another, the lonely and anxious young man could do nothing but wait for the arrival of one of the staff to answer his questions.

Is everything all right?

Is it a boy or a girl?

Is my wife all right?

Can I see her? Them?

What happens now?

He looked at his watch. Ten past four in the morning. He looked at the Firestone calendar pinned to the wall of faded and peeling wallpaper: Monday the twenty-eighth of July, nineteen thirty-six.

The long life of Barbara Mildred Conwyne had begun.

A little more than a month later — on Friday the fourth of September — baby Barbara's cousin was born to her mother's twin sister. However, that delivery was obstetrically different from Barbara's. It was completed on the same bed in the same Mount Eden nursing home supervised by a different but equally stern and spinsterish midwife at a late afternoon hour. The labour was long, difficult and painful, and left the new mother exhausted and resentful. And the result was not a strong, sturdy and healthy little girl but a boy child, big and bony, healthy enough, but born weak and exhausted as a result of his tortuous arrival. His birth caused his mother so much pain that she determined then, as she rejected her baby in order to sleep, to never have another child.

Unlike Barbara's father, the newborn boy's father had a wait of many hours — almost twenty-four of them — to get news of his wife and baby, unaware that the birth, from which he had been excluded, marked the virtual end of his marriage.

That, then, was the unhappy family into which fate delivered the baby William Edward Conwyne, cousin to Barbara.

The young cousins, Barbara and William, were not the only cousins in their family, but they were the only *young* ones, and the only ones in Auckland.

Their twin mothers — aged twenty-four when their children were born — were their own mother's late but happy and beloved "accidents", adored and utterly spoiled by their ageing, eccentric and wastrel father, Charles Edmund Brockley. They had an older brother, also Charles, who was then in his mid teens.

Although Charles the younger was born and raised in Auckland, by the time his young twin sisters had grown up and married, he, his wife Ruby and their children, were living in New Plymouth where Charles owned a Devon Street stationery shop, the largest in the city. His children, Cedric and Betty, were therefore in their teens when Barbara and William, their baby cousins in Auckland, were born.

Later, as a young man, William came to know his New Plymouth family well, especially his older cousin Cedric who became a good and close friend. Barbara, though, never met her New Plymouth family. She never wanted to.

For the first few years of the young cousins' lives their parents, and their two sets of Auckland-based grandparents — the Brockleys and Conwynes — were their family constants until war intervened and absented their fathers. As a result they grew closer to each other than most cousins not merely because they had only each other — their only and much older cousins living in distant New Plymouth — but more especially because their mothers, Mildred and Millicent (*née* Brockley) were identical twins while their fathers, Robert and Edward Conwyne, were brothers.

The young Conwyne families shared a rented house in Brockley Street, near where the brothers had grown up, in the shadow of Brockley Cottage where the twins had grown up. When the time came, therefore, Barbara and William started together at the same Mount Eden school where their parents — mothers and fathers — had once been students.

From the beginning it was generally believed, by most teachers and all students, that Barbara and William were sister and brother. It was an understandable, forgivable and harmless mistake. They had the same last name and, although William was taller than Barbara, they otherwise resembled each other in their refined good looks and personal mannerisms. Without conferring — they rarely did or had to — neither Barbara nor William said or did anything to dispel this common misapprehension. They were in fact pleased to be thought of as siblings.

Their parents and grandparents knew better but nevertheless considered their closeness — in appearance, behaviour and affection — to be charming and "cute", not noticing that as they grew older, and away from school, they tended to prefer each other's company over all others.

Only their maternal grandparents remembered that their identical twin daughters, Mildred and Millicent, so much younger than their only brother, had come to rely on each for company, a reliance that deepened as they grew until they purposely distanced themselves from other children to the point of being considered aloof and anti-social.

'A miracle those girls ever got married,' was a common sentiment.

It was assumed that if they hadn't married the neighbouring Conwyne brothers, who came from a working class family at the Mount Eden Road end of Brockley Street, they would have aged together in a shared spinsterhood.

As for the young Barbara and William, it shouldn't be assumed that they were anti-social, nor somehow deficient in social skills. Despite all they had in common they were not siblings but cousins; a girl and a boy who naturally carried within themselves — their minds and bodies — the natural feminine and masculine traits and preferences.

From their first days at primary school Barbara and William were both popular with their peers while their teachers and all adults found them to be consistently cheerful and polite. However, despite mixing and playing normally with other children at school they always walked home together, even holding hands in their primary school years. And, unless some other event or commitment intervened, they preferred to spend their evenings and weekends together.

During those carefree and innocent years at primary school, Barbara and William — naive about adult matters, as all children should be — were unaware that the world was at war and that their mothers, their mothers' family and their fathers' parents, were facing extraordinary worries and troubles.

William's father Edward was fighting overseas. Barbara's father Robert was stationed at Papakura military camp awaiting transfer to — the family believed — somewhere awful, dangerous and disease-ridden in the Middle East. As a result, Mildred and Millicent were permanently anxious, stressed by war and the absence of their husbands who they knew must have been in constant mortal danger.

To them — Mildred and Millicent — the world seemed to be engulfed in chaos, the vastness and complexity of which they couldn't begin to understand. They felt as though they no longer controlled their formerly small and uncomplicated lives and so fell back on their childhood habit of clinging interdependence, spending as much time together as they could. They even spent many of their otherwise lonely nights together with their parents and children in Brockley Cottage where they grew up.

Barbara and William therefore spent almost all their waking non-school hours in each other's company, and many of their sleeping hours together in one Brockley Cottage bed or the other. Always happy in each other's company, the children were the very least of their worried mothers' worries.

Of all this — the world at war and its traumatic impact on the adults of their family — Barbara and William knew nothing. Unaware of anything or anyone but themselves, they knew only that they naturally and unconsciously loved only their mothers and each other knowing, without doubt, that they were loved in return.

No one or nothing else mattered; their little lives were certain and simple, free of stress or anxiety.

They didn't know it then but would later look back on those war years with a sad and yearning nostalgia: just the two of them and their mothers, no fathers, supported — in the beginning at least — by two sets of loving grandparents.

Chapter 2

Early in nineteen forty-two, Barbara and William's shared paternal grandfather, a motorman on the trams, who would have been retired but for the war, died suddenly in his old Brockley Street villa. It happened one Saturday afternoon, while he was sitting in his armchair, listening to a rugby commentary on the wireless, waiting for his wife to bring him a cup of tea.

Near the end of the war, their maternal grandfather — the twins' eccentric and spendthrift father, Charles Edmund Brockley, who had always doted on his twin daughters but was estranged from his namesake son Charles — also died after a short illness brought about, it was said, by lack of sleep and the excessive consumption of whisky and tobacco. His widow, the children's maternal grandmother, then pleaded for one of her daughters — she didn't care which — to come back to Brockley Cottage to care for her as her health was failing, the unaffordable servants had all gone, and she couldn't alone manage the house and its three acres of land.

It was Mildred who left her nearby home, with Barbara, and moved in with her mother who died anyway, within a year. Mildred and little Barbara were then left to live alone in Brockley Cottage, the absurdly named Brockley family mansion.

Tragically, when the war in Europe was almost over, Mildred's husband Robert — Barbara's father — lost his life. *Killed in action,* they said. *Served with distinction. An important and decisive battle.*

Mildred had never heard of the battle; it wasn't important enough to be in the paper. She went to her grandfather's library, pulled down his huge *Chalmers's Own Modern Atlas of the World (including India, the colonies, and the Holy Land),* but couldn't find the tiny French village which gave its name to the battle in which her dear Robert had lost his life. But he was dead. Just thirty-five years old. Dead without doubt. But there was no body. No funeral. No grave. And so, for his wife, no hope.

The news, when conveyed to his already widowed and grieving old mother, brought about her sudden and unexplainable death.

Suddenly Barbara and William had no living grandparents.

Barbara, almost nine when her mother received the news of Robert's death, shared her mother's grief, not for the loss of her father, whom she barely remembered, but because she loved her mother dearly and hated to see her so wretchedly miserable. She tried to cheer her up, urging her to join William and his mother at the pictures where Robert used to work. But everything they saw there seemed to be about soldiers and war — even the comedies and musicals were about war — or romance.

The late Robert Conwyne had been a fine young man; a loving husband, devoted and faithful when many if not most young soldiers away at war surrendered to temptation knowing that any day could be their last and that any pleasure offered should therefore be taken "just in case". He left behind a wife, equally loving, devoted and faithful.

A husband missing in action made Mildred one of the most pitied and saddest widows of all. She would never have fully recovered without the support of her twin sister Millicent who, later, had to suffer her own but different loss. The result was to draw the twins even *closer* together, where they had been as children and where they remained, without husbands, for the rest of their lives.

William's father Edward did return from the war, physically unharmed but angry and bitter. He was unhappy in his marriage *before* he left and so, unlike his brother, had fornicated his way around various zones of war. But his carnal and frequently perverted excesses did nothing to relieve the horrors he saw inflicted by humans on humans in the name of one glorious cause or another.

Edward didn't exactly enjoy war but did appreciate the routines of army life; that his needs were provided for, decisions made for him. He had personal responsibility for nothing. And so he returned reluctantly to his Brockley Street home: to a wife who secretly wished that he and not his brother had been killed, and that she and not her sister was a widow; to a nine-year-old son, William, who hardly remembered him and for whom he felt nothing but resentment; and to his tedious eight-hour-a-day clerical job in the Mount Eden Borough Council rates department which took him back only because it was a legal obligation.

For the first six months at home Edward drank too much, with returned comrades, frequently coming home and abusing Millicent, forcing himself on her and so leaving her fretting about an unwanted pregnancy. He also frequently beat young William, with his army belt, for harmless and sometimes imagined childish misdemeanours.

William saw and experienced more violence in that six months than any boy should; he longed to protect his sometimes-bruised and always-frightened mother but was powerless against his heartless and angry father.

Millicent, though, was torn between hating Edward — before he left she had merely disliked him — and feeling sorry for him. She told Mildred that he woke every night screaming with fear as a result of what she called his "horrid nightmares".

'They're so awful he says he can't begin to tell me,' she confided.

The twins were seeing little of each other since Edward's return; he didn't approve of their closeness and how they had always shared intimate confidences while excluding him.

'But, Millie, look at your bruises,' said her shocked sister.

'It's not that bad. Not really.'

'But you can't put up with it,' insisted Mildred who was suddenly aware of what her brother-in-law must have become whilst away at war; aware of what her sister must have been quietly and secretly enduring. 'You just can't, Millie. You mustn't.'

'He's trying hard,' said Millicent, gently rubbing her bruised arm. 'And, anyway, now that you and Barbara aren't there he sleeps in your room.'

'But when he drinks. When he drinks…'

'Most of the time he's all right. Just goes to his room and sleeps it off.'

'And what about poor little William?'

'He's all right most of the time. He just keeps out of his way.'

In fact, though, Millicent was secretly frightened for her little boy's sake as well as her own. She often cried, alone at night, when she thought of what her brave little chap had to endure in the home where he and she together had hitherto been safe, secure and happy.

One morning in November, on the way to school, Barbara noticed — she couldn't not — that William's left eye was partly closed, and that the flesh around it was variously dark-blue and a yellowish-brown.

'Is it your dad, again, William? Did he do it?'

William nodded grimly.

The cousins often discussed the red strap-welts on the back of William's calves, or high on his thighs, and even higher where he was too embarrassed to show Barbara, but he had never been bruised about the head and face before; not as far as Barbara knew.

'Does Auntie Millie know?'

'She said I've gotta say I walked into the toilet door in the dark,' said William. 'If they ask me.'

'But it *was* your dad, wasn't it?'

William nodded again. His eye hurt a lot. He wanted to cry but didn't.

Barbara so wanted to stop and hug William, to comfort him and perhaps relieve his pain just as she was used to comforting her mother to perhaps help relieve her pain.

Secretly, in return, William longed to be hugged by Barbara. His mother didn't hug him any more and he didn't know why.

'I think it's awful what your dad does,' said Barbara. 'So does Mummy.'

'I *hate* him,' said William angrily; he had to work hard again not to cry.

'Let me see properly.'

They stopped and William bent forward a little to let Barbara have a close look. She inspected the eye closely and reached up slowly meaning to gently touch William's cheek. But William winced in anticipation and pulled away.

Barbara quickly drew back her hand.

'I'm sorry, William,' she said kindly. 'True dinks. I really and truly am.'

William looked at Barbara's close face. He was glad she knew about his father; how awful he was. And he secretly wished he had let Barbara touch his cheek.

By the end of that year, nineteen forty-five, when the war was over, Edward Conwyne's hot temper had cooled. It was as if he was literally exhausted by the effort it took to be always angry. Millicent cooked him breakfast each morning, and prepared a hot and nourishing meal each night which he shared, at the table, with her and William. But he was surly and ungrateful. And there was no conversation between them.

Thursday nights he handed Millicent his wages and then left it to her to manage their finances just as she had done for the years he was away. He went often to the RSA, where he had a lot of friends and comrades, or sometimes to a pub in town. But although he often came home drunk, there was, by then, no anger, no violence, no anything.

Christmas came and went. But there was no joy, only sadness, in each of the Conwyne homes. The twin mothers were kept apart by the jealous, suspicious and sullen — but no longer angry or violent — Edward.

Then, during the long summer school holidays of nineteen forty-six, Edward suddenly, unexpectedly, became meek and compliant, a nervous ex-serviceman, utterly lacking energy and motivation. And whereas in the months following his return, even as recently as Christmas, he had expressed his disapproval of Mildred's close emotional ties to her twin sister, a closeness he recognized and envied, he surrendered to the inevitable, no longer caring that she spent more time at Brockley Cottage with her sister than at home with him.

Wherever Millicent went, there too went William.

'The boy needs to be with young blokes his own age,' Edward used to protest angrily to Millicent. 'He spends too much time with that girl.'

But now, resigned, he didn't seem to care.

Even at his young age William could see that his father was a sad and empty man, his morale destroyed by the war he refused to discuss, who deserved sympathy more than scorn and, above all, was now no longer to be feared. And so, during that summer holiday, the little group of four — the twin mothers and their children, Barbara and William — resumed their wartime habit of spending all their time together although, now, mostly at Brockley Cottage to avoid any contact at all with the moody and unpleasant, if harmless, Edward.

Edward, for his part, having quietly spent months brooding over his situation, decided to sell his parents' now vacant home, which he alone had inherited, and altogether abandon his wife and son. He left nothing of the proceeds to either his wife or his grieving and deserving sister-in-law. It was thought by his RSA comrades that he had gone bush in the South Island while his relieved colleagues at the council believed he had gone to Australia.

Whatever the truth, Edward Conwyne was never seen again. Years later, Millicent was notified of his death.

Chapter 3

Edward's disappearance, and the death of all the children's grandparents, meant that by the middle of nineteen forty-six the twin sisters and their two children were alone in Auckland. The sisters' older brother and his family in New Plymouth were naturally preoccupied with their own affairs and troubles including the loss of one of Ruby's brothers — not more than a boy — in the Pacific war. They, in New Plymouth, were thus unaware and uncaring of the plight of Charles's younger twins sisters in Auckland, and their children, as they always had been.

'It's just you and me and the kids now, Millie,' said Mildred, Barbara's still-sad mother, to her sister.

'Oh, Millie,' said her sister, 'isn't it awful.'

But Millicent didn't really think it was awful at all. Once she knew Edward was truly gone, that he had sold his parents' house, she quickly joined her sister at Brockley Cottage taking a happy William to join his cousin Barbara.

'We're home together again,' said Mildred. 'And we still have each other.'

'And the children are happy,' added Millicent.

'They *are* happy, aren't they,' said Mildred. 'That's the main thing. The children are happy.'

Barbara and William *were* happy.

They were happy living together with their mothers and each other. And although Barbara's mother still missed Robert, she gradually became adjusted to her widowhood which she carried bravely with the support of her sister. Barbara, meanwhile, didn't miss the father she remembered only faintly while William and his mother were openly glad to be without Edward.

The next year passed happily for the four Conwynes. The twin mothers lived easily in each other's company, free of conflict, sharing everything including their work and worries as well as their joys. They resumed dressing the same, wearing the same clothes, shoes and other accessories, doing their hair the same, as they always had before they had husbands and children. They knew each other intimately; could read each other's thoughts as only twins can and do.

Barbara and William, too, were utterly content. They had everything young children need: they were always warm, comfortable and well-nourished in a safe, familiar and unchanging environment steeped in family history, surrounded by the unconditional love of two mothers. They went to school and returned together, and spent all their time at home together — after school, on the weekends and during the school holidays — needing no other friends or company. And even when Barbara was being a girl, playing with her dolls, playing house, or learning to knit or sew or bake or cook from her mother and aunt, and William was spending boy hours on the floor with his Meccano set, or Hornby train or his Dinky Toys car collection, they were still in the same house, a fact which comforted them both.

That a young girl and boy should be so comfortable in each other's company, needing no other friends of their own sex, might have seemed strange under normal circumstances, in a conventional mother-and-father family. But to the twin mothers, raised by their loving mother and spoiled by their idle father, now without the influence of a husband, and unmoved by any outside opinion, their children's peculiarly close relationship seemed merely to mirror their own. It appeared — to them at least — to be perfectly healthy and natural.

Modest and pleasant renown came to the twin mothers the next year.

In nineteen forty-eight Barbara and William started at Kōwhai Intermediate school. Their mothers believed they were old enough to look after themselves after school allowing them — Mildred and Millicent — to look for a job they could do together. And so they began working as waitresses in the Farmers rooftop cafeteria.

The Farmers was the country's largest department store and its rooftop cafeteria, adjacent to the toy department — home of Hector, the store's cockatoo mascot — and the children's rooftop playground, was famous for its elegant *art-deco* décor, refined ambience, huge goldfish tank, starched white table cloths, silver cutlery and tea services, fine china, and a vast range of delicate cakes, pastries and sandwiches. The elegantly-dressed, -gloved, -hatted and mostly wealthy lady customers were served by waitresses uniformed in a black dress, a frilled white apron and lace cap, the prettiest and friendliest of whom were — everyone agreed — the thirty-five-year-old twin Conwyne sisters. Their identical looks, as well as their friendliness, prettiness and efficiency, made them a unique attraction which frequently brought them to the attention of the photographers of *The Auckland Star, The Weekly News* and *The New Zealand Woman's Weekly*. It also drew unsubtle advances from many of their male colleagues, some of the company's directors, and many other wealthy men. Romantic advances were always politely rejected by both women: Millicent because her only experience with a man — her husband, William's father — was so unpleasant; Mildred because her only experience with a man — her late husband, Barbara's father — was so loving that she believed it could never be repeated; to even try would be an insult to her Robert's memory.

Waitressing at the Farmers was the ideal job for the twins as the café was open only during the day, and only for morning tea, lunch and afternoon tea, weekdays only — at that time in New Zealand no shops were open on the weekend — which meant they, as dutiful mothers, could see Barbara and William off to school and be home in time to make tea, as the evening meal was then called. Barbara and William were therefore alone together in the house after school until their mothers got home about five o'clock.

After tea in the summer the children played together outside, on an ancient swing their grandfather Brockley had erected (not for them but for their mothers when young), or in the tree hut (built by the same grandfather for the same children) in the huge monkey apple tree at the far end of the back yard bordering the Maungawhau park. And in the winter, bathed and ready for bed, they lay, sprawled out on the carpet in front of the parlour fire, reading comics or colouring-in together until it was time for bed. And although they each started the night, happy and secure, in their own bedroom, their own bed, they often woke in the morning, together, in one or the other's bed.

Their mothers thought it was "sweet" that the cousins, their children, should love each other so.

By the end of nineteen forty-eight the two mothers and two children had been living together in Brockley Cottage for two years. During that time Barbara and William's mutual loyalty and dependence had ripened beyond childhood affection. Neither could understand their own feelings, let alone express them to each other, nor discuss them with anyone — including their mothers — but by the time Barbara's womanhood arrived they were not only sleeping together often, for part of the night, for comfort and company, but also, sometimes, sleeping in each other's embrace until morning.

Chapter 4

It was on the last such night, when William, lying languidly on his side, curled closely behind Barbara and put his arm around her waist. Only half awake, he instinctively drew her close, pressing his young hardness against her pyjamaed thigh. Barbara responded drowsily, naturally, in her own way. With an innocence to equal William's, she pushed back with soft and encouraging sighs. They acted with tenderness — a natural expression of their feelings for each other — without speaking, without embarrassment, until, overcome with pleasure, they drifted together into a blissful sleep filled with what could be described only as genuine adult love.

Unfortunately, coincidentally, Barbara's first female release came that night, as she slept in William's arms. Her discovery in the morning — she woke early, at dawn, waking William in the process — not only frightened and horrified her but caused William to believe that it was somehow his fault; that he had, in some unknown and mysterious way, done something wrong — evil even — to somehow grievously wound his beloved cousin. He fled from her room to the bathroom, to quickly cleanse himself of his own mysterious stickiness, before dashing back on tip-toes to the cold sheets of his own bed where he lay for more than an hour listening to Barbara and her mother's murmured and muffled conversation.

William was surprised that his aunt sounded kind, sympathetic somehow, not at all angry. That reassured him. And then, distantly, from along the hall, he heard the bath being run, and realized that

Barbara was being helped by her mother to wash away the blood which had so horrified them both.

'Barbara's curse has arrived,' said Mildred. She and Millicent were on the tram, going to work.

'Oh, Millie,' said Millicent. 'Poor thing.'

'Had to come, I suppose.'

'She's early though, isn't she? Earlier than us.'

Mildred shrugged. 'Who knows these days.'

It wasn't a question. The war and widowhood had left Mildred confused about many things.

'So, three of us now,' said Millicent. 'Imagine it. All together.'

Mildred shrugged. 'Nuns in a convent they say.'

'She *knows* everything I suppose,' said Millicent. 'All the doings? Babies and that?'

'She does now,' said Mildred, nodding. 'I had to tell her didn't I.'

'But what about William?' said Millicent. 'I haven't told him anything. I mean, it's a father's job isn't it. But where's *he* when he's needed. What do you say to a boy? So embarrassing.'

'I wouldn't worry,' said Mildred. 'Boys seem to get everything they need from other boys. Friends and that. They talk about that stuff all the time, boys.'

'But William hasn't got any friends,' said Millicent. 'Not really. Only Barbara.'

They didn't speak for a while until Millicent, struck by a sudden thought, said hopefully: 'Maybe Barbara will tell him everything.'

Mildred turned at looked at her sister, wide-eyed in disbelief.

'About boys?' she said. 'I doubt it. And, anyway, she's gone right off the subject. Since it happened I mean. They definitely won't sleep together any more. Not if she's got anything to do with it.'

'Oh, my goodness,' said Millicent. 'Poor William. He hasn't said anything about it. Not to me. Not a word.'

'Well, he wouldn't, would he,' said Mildred. 'I think they were both horrified. I know Barbara was.'

Barbara and William *were* horrified. Barbara especially so. But not for the reason assumed by her mother. Her original horror subsided to be replaced by misinformed worry and fear. Worry and fear which unfortunately came to blight her life.

And William's.

For that summer, and the whole of the following year, William avoided Barbara as much as he could. He was awkward, embarrassed and guilty, still believing he had done something to physically hurt Barbara. He desperately wanted to ask her how she was. Was it painful? Had she healed? Did she have to go to the doctor? Would she have to go to hospital for an operation?

Above all he wanted to apologize. He wanted to hold her close, hug her, and tell her that he was sorry and that it would never happen again. But he simply couldn't find the words — what shy twelve-year-old boy ever could? — and so he tried to pretend it didn't happen, that it would go away and be forgotten.

But he *couldn't* forget and would lie awake at night, remembering first how wonderful it once was to lie with Barbara for hours, sleeping peacefully through an entire night. And then he'd grimace, curling his toes, as he remembered what had happened that night; what he had done.

He did recall, happily and with temporary relief, that he wasn't alone. That Barbara had joined him, whispered his name, again and again. But then the horror and shame returned when he remembered, later, when she woke him up, showed him the blood. His toes curled again then, involuntarily, with embarrassment and shame.

Oh, how he longed to talk to her about it. How he wished they could be friends again — despite what he had done, despite the hurt and pain he must have caused — while assuming they never could.

Meanwhile, Barbara was puzzled. She couldn't understand what she had done to make William act so strangely. She wanted to tell him that her mother had explained everything about that morning, about periods and sex and boys and having babies, and had apologized for not telling her sooner, for not warning her about what might — *would* — happen to her and all girls about her age and what to do about it. She had explained it so plainly and simply that Barbara wanted to explain it to William, exactly that way, if only she could. But just as he couldn't find a way to ask how she was, she couldn't find a way to open the subject; to ask what was wrong with him. Them. Why wouldn't he talk to her any more? What had she done? If she knew she would be glad to apologize and explain everything.

It was an awful year for them both. Two young people, cousins, close friends all their lives, suddenly unable to chat innocently about anything, unable to spend happy hours together, as they once had, talking casually about nothing. Unable to recapture the guilt-free simpleness of childhood. Trapped awkwardly, instead, in the confused, self-conscious, tongue-tied clumsiness of adolescence.

Meanwhile their mothers took no particular notice of their changed behaviour. They thought and agreed that "the children" were probably going through a "phase".

Chapter 5

Things changed the next year thanks to Barbara's growing maturity. She was, like all girls, more mature in every way than any boy her own age, and certainly more mature than her cousin. By then William had joined a circle of school friends who had little in common but their gaucheness, forced coarse language and utter ignorance about sex and what girls thought and wanted. He was often uncomfortable in the company of these new friends, and with their frequently uncouth behaviour, but was too mild-mannered to object and, anyway, without them he would have no company at all.

The truth was — he had to admit it to himself, when he reluctantly thought about — that Barbara was the only friend he wanted. She was the only person in whose company he was, or once was, perfectly at ease. He knew she was perfectly happy to spend quiet hours at Brockley Cottage with him, inside, or exploring the old stables, potting shed and greenhouse, even sometimes playing on the swings together. He knew, with relief, she would never shamelessly parade herself in front of him and his *ersatz* friends, as some girls did, at the milk bars of Queen Street, or outside the Crystal Palace or the picture theatres in Dominion Road.

It helped — or perhaps *didn't* help — that he and Barbara no longer went to school together.

In nineteen fifty, the year the British Empire Games were held at Eden Park, Barbara started at Epsom Girls' Grammar while

William went to Auckland Grammar, a boys-only school. They left for school separately, at different times, and returned, separately and at different times, for the first time in their school lives. But they still came home to uncomfortably share an empty house for a few hours.

Late one afternoon, in the middle of that first year at high school, Barbara interrupted William at his homework to ask him if they could have a proper heart-to-heart talk. She was standing in the doorway of his bedroom which was upstairs, next to hers, above the ballroom. She was wearing an apron over her school uniform and holding a potato-peeler as she was about to start preparing dinner.

William's heart ached with love for her. He turned to face her — he was sitting at his desk — trying to appear nonchalant and politely attentive. He thought she looked beautiful.

'I've really hated it that we've forgotten how to be proper friends, William,' he heard her say. 'And I don't know why.'

'Neither do I,' said William awkwardly and untruthfully. Despite appearances he felt anxious and uncertain. To him, Barbara seemed older and more self-assured.

'Well, can't we talk about it? Heart to heart?'

'I suppose so,' said William who managed to sound resigned to the inevitable, reluctant, but was in fact nervously excited by the possibility of repairing his relationship with the only person in the world who had ever been a real friend; his best friend; his only friend. And he was also excited, as he'd never been before, that his lovely cousin, looking so pretty, demure and domestic, was again on the threshold of his bedroom.

'So can I come in?'

William nodded. Thrilled. He put down his pencil, closed the atlas which had been the object of his study, and turned fully in his chair to face Barbara who was by then sitting on the edge of his bed. He felt nervous, as though his voice would shake if he spoke.

He tried hard to relax; to appear blasé.

'What happened, William, you know what I mean. Last year. Before Christmas. It wasn't your fault.'

'I know,' said William casually although he didn't know. He hoped his voice sounded normal.

'So why have you been acting so funny and that? I don't get it.'

William shrugged.

'Do you know anything about girls, William? About their periods and things like that?'

'Course I do,' said William trying hard to look and sound nonchalant knowing his knowledge of Barbara's subject was crude, probably wrong and certainly incomplete.

'You *do* know that what happened to me that night wasn't your fault,' Barbara said rather than asked. 'You didn't hurt me or anything. You do know that that don't you? Really for sure?'

William merely nodded. He felt as if he had blushed and hoped Barbara hadn't notice. She *did* notice although she didn't mention it. With a woman's intuition she realized then — suddenly — that while she was speaking from experience, with a woman's voice, William was hearing with the ear and understanding of a naive boy. With that realization — knowing also that William *would* one day properly understand, and soon she hoped — she decided to retreat from her plan which had been based on the mistaken assumption that William was her age in his head as well as his body.

And so, retreating, she simply said: 'Well, then, there's nothing to worry about is there?'

'S'pose not,' said William, still a bit confused. He'd expected more from what Barbara had called a "heart-to-heart" talk.

'So why don't we become good friends again?' Barbara asked. 'Like we used to. Do nice things together.'

William wasn't at all sure he could ever again be merely a friend of his lovely cousin who, still dressed in her school uniform and apron, was sitting on the edge of his bed. Her hands were in her lap, holding her potato-peeler, her head tilted to one side. She was smiling kindly. She looked beautiful. He still felt nervous.

'All right,' he said, his cursory response hiding his relief that Barbara was evidently all right and didn't blame him for anything. 'I don't mind.'

And with the same womanly wisdom which had recognized the cause of William's boyish unease, Barbara rightly sensed the concealed happiness in his lukewarm response.

'That's good then, William. I'm glad.'

'Me too,' said William.

Barbara stood up then. 'Well, I better go downstairs. Get on with tea,' she said. 'Sausages tonight. They'll be home soon, eh.'

The next three years passed pleasantly and uneventfully for the four residents of Brockley Cottage. By then, the end of nineteen fifty-two, Barbara and William had settled into an agreeable relationship in which they talked comfortably about anything except — as if by unspoken agreement — how they *really* felt about each other. Meanwhile they had both done well at school, each easily passing their fifth form School Certificate.

They were ready for the long summer holiday after which they both planned to return to school for the sixth form.

In the meantime Barbara had entirely lost her girlish looks and demeanour. When dressed for a shopping trip to town, or for the pictures, with some light make-up, she might easily have been mistaken for a smart young secretary of nineteen or twenty years. She was, indeed, truly beautiful, a fact that did not escape men many years her senior but served only to intimidate boys her own age.

William, though, while not intimidated by her undeniable beauty — he knew her too well — sadly assumed that, when the time came, she would have her pick of Auckland's rich, handsome and eligible young men and would lose interest in him. That thought troubled him although he knew he had no special claim on her affections, and that to be jealous was foolish and unreasonable.

In this and everything else, he, too, had matured remarkably. Not only was he now strikingly tall, lean and muscular, deep-voiced and hairy — needing a daily shave — but had also matured intellectually, acquiring a manly confidence and self-assurance in the process. As a result he no longer sought the dubious company of boys he now considered foolish and immature. And, above all, as far as his former anxieties were concerned, he had learned properly — a little from his science lessons, a little more from a kindly school matron — that what had happened to his darling Barbara, as he secretly referred to her, that long-ago night, when she became a woman, and every month since, was entirely natural, nothing to be ashamed of nor embarrassed by. And certainly not the result of anything done by him to her.

Before, when Barbara had tried to have her "heart-to-heart" talk, when he was not quite fourteen years old, he was embarrassed by his ignorance compared with her knowledge and experience. But now, when he felt perfectly capable of discussing that night, that event, and his immature reaction to it, he felt embarrassed for a different set of reasons. Now, if they did have another genuine "heart-to-heart" talk, he was afraid he'd reveal not his boyish ignorance but his knowledge and understanding of her, of life, of himself, and how and why he loved her deeply, as a man loves a woman; how he dreamed that she might love him equally in return.

He thought such a talk would probably never happen. That he could hope for no more from Barbara than the cousinly affection and care she evidently preferred.

Barbara, however, loved, admired and desired her big, strong, kind and handsome cousin almost more than she could bear, more than she dared admit, and certainly as much as he loved and desired her. Foolishly, sadly for them both, Barbara's secret fear was the same as William's: that if she confessed her love to him it would not be returned. She knew she couldn't bear that.

And so, in the hope that one day in the future William might feel the same as she, she continued to deflect the attention she received from other young men.

Barbara and William's friendship therefore continued to appear to others — including their mothers — to be that of a close sister and brother. Maintaining that illusion, to each other as well as to others, was secretly and often excruciatingly difficult for them both.

Neither knew it was a difficulty they shared.

In nineteen fifty-two there was a series of important birthday parties: in July for Barbara's sixteenth, in September for William's sixteenth, and on the Saturday after Boxing Day for the twin mothers' shared fortieth.

Barbara's party was a small affair — just three of her best girlfriends from school — while William's was no more than a dinner at home cooked by Barbara with special attention to William's likes. But the twin mothers celebrated in an uncharacteristic fashion — without precedence and never to be repeated — with a party in the Brockley Cottage ballroom. It was the biggest party held in the old and sprawling Mount Eden mansion since their father's notoriously extravagant jazz parties of the nineteen-twenties.

It was at that unusual party, on a warm and humid Saturday night, that Barbara and William came to see how popular their mothers were with their Farmers colleagues, management and staff, old and young, male and female, as well with their customers.

'Forty, Millie,' shouted Millicent over the sound of the small orchestra. 'I can't believe it.'

They were at the bar for another fashionable Pimm's.

'Life begins now,' replied Mildred.

'What, dear? Didn't hear.'

'Life begins at forty,' shouted Mildred again. 'That's what they say.'

'And wouldn't Daddy have loved this,' said Millicent conspiratorially in her sister's ear as she waved her free long-gloved arm to take in the sight of a ballroom full of happy dancing people. 'A proper old-fashioned jamboree.'

Mildred merely giggled tipsily.

The sisters were definitely enjoying life at forty. They were single, had no commitments, a job they enjoyed, with lots of friends. And, above all, they agreed, it was good to see Barbara and William growing up happy, healthy and well adjusted.

Chapter 6

During the school holidays of that summer, Barbara and William were no longer left at home to look after themselves.

Barbara worked through the holidays for the Davenports, owners of a busy dairy in Balmoral. It was an almost full-time job caring for the two young Davenport children — a primary school boy and girl — as their parents were busy all day and into the evening. The family lived in a flat above the shop which had a small enclosed yard at the back. Barbara was left to prepare the children's lunch and afternoon snacks, and otherwise amuse them either at home or take them to the Potter's Park playground or even, sometimes, to one of the local afternoon picture shows for children. And if the dairy were especially busy in the late afternoon and evening, Mrs Davenport might ask her to prepare, or begin to prepare, the family's evening meal. Indeed, her lady employer was especially pleased with and impressed by sixteen-year-old Barbara's skill in the kitchen as well as her kind management of the children.

Barbara enjoyed her holiday job with the Davenports because Mr and Mrs Davenport treated her not as a schoolgirl but as a mature, capable and reliable young woman worthy of their trust. She was also well paid and managed to save almost all her wages.

She liked to see her savings grow and so decided not to return to school but to somehow find a permanent full-time job.

William's holiday job was pumping petrol and generally helping out at Collet's garage in the Mount Eden village. He enjoyed the work, frequently taking a good-humoured ribbing from the mechanics rostered to work over the holidays and who, in the process, happily passed on a little about motor car maintenance and repairs.

He enjoyed mixing daily with adult men; a new experience. He saw that they were knowledgeable tradesmen, appreciated and well-rewarded for their experience and skill, and yet otherwise completely natural and unaffected, neither especially crude nor prudish. Mr Collet called them "salt of the bloody earth Kiwis".

William sat with the men at what they called "smoko" — they all smoked — sharing tea and biscuits, morning and afternoon. He silently listened to their talk and banter about politics — they seemed to despise Sid Holland, the prime minister — and sport (mostly cricket, rugby and horse racing), their wives and in-laws, their children, and their frequently lewd jokes which he enjoyed knowing he could never share them with his mother, aunt or Barbara. He also learned, from Mr Collet, about dealing with customers, and from Mrs Collet about handling money, giving change, and even a little bookkeeping.

At the end of the day he was usually too tired to go out and so, like Barbara, he managed to save almost all his wages. By the end of the holidays he knew he liked working with men, earning and saving money, and so decided, like Barbara but without conferring, to not return to school. He decided to ask Mr Collet if he'd take him on as an apprentice motor mechanic.

Barbara and William rarely saw each other during those busy holidays. When they did, on the weekends especially, they usually spoke only of their holiday job experiences. They both enjoyed being treated as adults by adults, being free of school routines — including having to wear a uniform — getting a weekly wage and watching their savings grow.

What they didn't admit to each other — they could hardly admit it to themselves — was that being busy all day, sometimes into the evening, being out in the world, mixing with other people, kept each distracted from longing for the company of the other.

What they *did* admit to each other, but only when the holidays were over, was their common decision, but reached independently, to leave school and look for a job.

As his holiday job was coming to an end William asked Mr Collet about an apprenticeship.

'Sorry, boy,' said Mr Collet.

Mr Collet's existing apprentice still had a year to serve.

'Only big enough for one apprentice at a time,' explained a sympathetic Mrs Collet.

William was disappointed. He had enjoyed his holiday job at Collet's and had come to like and be liked by the men there. But he didn't relish having to meet and mix with a new group of men in another workshop.

He remembered then that one of the managers at Farmers — whom he had met at the twins' big fortieth birthday party — had promised his mother and aunt that either or both their young ones would be welcome to work at Farmers. He said they were fine young people. Just the kind of people the firm needed for the future.

'I'll find them a good job, Millie,' William had heard him say, somewhat slurringly. 'You just say the word, my love. Just say the word.'

Millicent arranged an appointment for William with the important Farmers man in question. William found him — a constant cigar smoker — to be so fat that he seemed to be bursting out of his tightly stretched button-popping waistcoat, so jolly that he found everything to be a bit of fun, but not very helpful as far as offering a motor mechanic apprenticeship.

'Our shop, lad,' he said, referring to the company's motor garage. 'Only our own trucks and vans. Deliveries etcetera. Three senior mechanics. Army trained. All we need. No apprentices. Sorry, lad. However...' he added as he reached for his phone.

William was escorted across Hobson Street by a young man in an inky khaki overall who said his name was Barry and that he was nearly finished his printing apprenticeship.

'I suppose you'll be replacing me,' he said.

There, in a large, noisy and fumy factory, William was interviewed by the manager and foreman of the Farmers printing department. He left, after the two-man interview and an hour-long tour, with a fat and folded "Contract of Apprenticeship" in his pocket to be signed by his parent or guardian.

Barbara, too, was offered a job at Farmers.

'Mummy, I don't want to work at Farmers,' she insisted.

'Darling girl,' said Mildred, 'it's a wonderful chance. The biggest department store in the country. Really. A good job just waiting for you. Any department you like he said.'

'But doing what?' asked Barbara resentfully. 'Serving customers all day. Stuck behind a counter. Might as well work in Davenport's dairy. No thanks.'

Mildred was disappointed but Barbara was determined. She knew what she wanted thanks to the talks with Mrs Davenport. They were usually brief talks — Mrs Davenport was always busy in the shop — but they were insightful and unfailingly helpful, laced with more worldly wisdom and sensible advice than Barbara knew she would ever receive from her flighty, inexperienced and unserious mother.

It was as a result of Mrs Davenport's advice that Barbara used much of her savings to enrol in a twelve-week course at the Wakefield-Trident Secretarial College.

'You've done typing at school, and bookkeeping, so it makes sense,' said Mrs Davenport. 'You'll learn Pitman's, too,' she added. 'With your looks and personality and grooming you're sure to get a good well-paid job in any modern business. Believe me, Barbara, a lot better than serving in a shop. And I know all about that don't I.'

A little more than three months later — having topped her class at Wakefield-Trident, earning a glowing testimonial from her tutors — seventeen-year-old Barbara successfully applied for a junior secretarial position at Smith and Brown, a large and prestigious furniture store at the top of Symonds Street.

By then, the end of July, nineteen fifty-three, William had successfully completed and passed his apprenticeship probation at Farmers and was on the way to being a qualified letterpress printer.

Barbara was in the noisy Smith and Brown typing pool for a little more than two years. And then, at the end of nineteen fifty-five she was promoted to the hushed and carpeted executive suite as personal secretary to one of the firm's directors, and the soft furnishings buyer, old Mr Simmonite; she had just turned nineteen.

Meanwhile, despite his early misgivings about starting a new job and meeting new people, William had successfully settled into his work. His calm, gentle and unassuming nature, combined with his willingness to take directions, learn, and work hard, meant he was liked and welcomed by both his colleagues and managers. He found that the congenial workplace, with men, young and old, who had quickly become friends, easily satisfied his yearning for a reassuring routine.

Thus did the cousins begin to live separate lives. They left and returned home at different times, spent their work-days at different places where they made different friends and established different routines. Even their weekends were spent mostly apart.

But whatever they were doing, wherever and with whom, they each continued to secretly wish they were doing something else, somewhere else, with the other.

William, no longer a boy, assumed the role of "man of the house", catching up with maintenance of the house and garden, both of which had fallen into disrepair since his grandfather Brockley had died. He realized that his mother and aunt, who now owned Brockley Cottage — their older brother Charles having long ago been cut from his father's will — and Barbara too for that matter, had no idea of the work required to maintain such an old and large wooden house and keep its grounds in order.

William could see all that needed doing — some urgently — and so set about it all methodically, energetically, thoroughly, evenings and weekends, which meant he spent very little time with the women of the house. Being busy all week at work, and keeping himself busy at home, helped keep his mind off Barbara.

While he always felt dirty, with ink-stained hands during the week, and dust and dirt, oil and paint, on the weekends, he thought Barbara always looked beautifully groomed, her hair always in place, her make-up perfect and her clothes looking new, fresh, clean and colourful, even when she was helping with housework, cooking, cleaning and washing.

And, it seemed to him, and unlike him, she had a busy social life, always going somewhere with friends during weekends, being called on at night by a different young man with a nice car, to go to a party, the pictures or a dance.

Hurt and jealous, William did his best to be somewhere else when one of Barbara's invariably charming, handsome and smartly-dressed young men arrived. But sometimes he couldn't avoid being introduced. When that happened he felt unclean, untidy and inadequate, quickly wiping his hands down on his old trousers before shaking hands politely with Barbara's new escort while she stood at his side looking unbelievably beautiful. It hurt him grievously that Barbara seemed happy to be going out somewhere new and exciting with this new and evidently exciting young man while being unaware of his own discomfort and unhappiness.

His feelings were hurt further when, first, he had to stand on the front veranda alone to watch her skipping down the gravel drive, laughing and joking, as she got into the sort of car he thought he could never afford. And again, the next morning at breakfast, when she excitedly told her mother and aunt where she had been, whom she had met there, and perhaps about the supper and the orchestra, and the gowns worn by all the beautiful glamorous girls.

It was information that fascinated the listening mothers but merely saddened William who often left the table with a weak excuse rather than listen any more than demanded by courtesy.

William easily understood why Barbara was so attractive to other young men but he didn't understand why she was so attracted to *them*. They all seemed so pretentious.

He'd never met a girl who interested him as much as Barbara did and so had no interest in dating any other women, even if only for company. His social life was limited, by choice, to a few after-work beers with his colleagues or going to the pictures with his mother and aunt.

Chapter 7

The uneasy atmosphere at Brockley Cottage, between Barbara and William but barely noticed by their vague and preoccupied mothers, was broken at the end of nineteen fifty-six with a long-overdue discussion. It was initiated by Barbara as a result of an official-looking letter — OHMS — to William commanding him to report to the army for compulsory military training.

At that time all twenty-year-old men were required to undertake three months military service. Having turned twenty in September, William was expecting the summons. But Barbara was surprized and worried.

While her initiative should have been a relief to William, it was a discussion with unfortunate and long-term consequences for them both.

Barbara learned about the letter not from William but, later, from her mother.

'When?' she asked William.

She found him working in the potting shed. She was wearing a denim overall. Her hair was tied up with a red scarf. She was wearing no make-up. William thought she looked wonderful.

He was glad to see her in *his* domain for a change.

'Have to have a medical first,' he said. 'Have to report to Rutland Street next week.'

'And then?'

'First thing next year, I suppose,' he said. 'Middle of January I think.'

'For how long?'

'Just three months,' said William.

'Oh, *William*,' said Barbara. She sounded despondent. 'You'll be away all summer.'

William was somehow glad but surprized that Barbara sounded so unhappy. She must know, he thought, that all men get called up when they turn twenty.

'It'll go quick enough,' he said, trying to sound unconcerned. 'That's what the blokes at work say. Doesn't take long.'

'Will you write?'

'Course I will,' he said. 'If I'm allowed.'

'They *must* let you write.'

'I suppose so.'

'Oh, William, I *will* miss you.'

William was surprised again. Amazed even.

'Will you *really*?'

'Of *course* I will,' said Barbara somewhat indignantly. 'Are you all right, William?' she added with a puzzled look.

William thought she looked especially lovely then. Looking puzzled suited her.

'Why?' he asked. 'What do you mean?'

'Well, I worry about you sometimes.'

Barbara was thinking then of William, her little boy cousin, being beaten by his angry soldier father, now having to himself train as a soldier. How, she wondered, would he manage? Would there be bullies in the army? Would he cope? And what about all the guns and danger?

'Why?' William was genuinely puzzled.

Barbara suddenly saw again the grown-up William. A boy no longer. An athletic young man, looking fit and strong, standing straight and tall at the work bench, his short sleeves revealing tanned and muscular arms. A confident, self-reliant young man obviously capable of looking after himself amongst other men. How foolish, she felt, to think otherwise.

'I don't know,' she said meekly. 'Just being silly I suppose.'

But she was still worried. About something else. So she asked again: 'Are you *sure* everything's all right, William?'

'Yes,' insisted William. 'Why do you keep asking me that?'

'Well, I don't know. You just don't seem to have any fun. Don't go out or anything.'

'I go out plenty,' said William. 'Go to the pictures with Mother and Aunt Millie every week.'

Barbara screwed up her face in mild disgust. Going to the pictures with the twin mothers was something she now never did.

'That's not what I mean,' she said. 'You don't seem to have any friends.'

'Tennis club,' said William. 'I'm on the committee now. Lots of pals at the tennis club.'

'But what about *girls*, William?'

'Lots of girls too.'

'I don't mean *that*, William. I mean you don't have a special girl. A proper girlfriend. Someone you really like.'

William, feeling bold only because he was soon going away and might never have a better chance to say what he thought, what he really felt, looked directly into his questioning companion's eyes, and said, so plainly that his meaning could *never* be misunderstood: 'To be honest, Barbara, the only girl I've ever liked — I mean loved, really *loved* — is you, actually. There'll never be anyone else. Honestly.'

Barbara was suddenly overwhelmed with emotion, with love for her dear cousin.

'Oh, *William*,' she said in a rush, almost ready to cry. She joined her hands and brought them up to her face as if praying. 'I know what you mean, William. I really do.'

She paused then, hunched her shoulders and pushed her hands into her big pockets.

'The thing is,' she added, taking the plain-speaking lead from William, 'well, I really love you too. *Only* you. None of those others. Really. Just you.'

William was amazed and thrilled by her confession.

'But, William,' she said, 'it's *hopeless*. Absolutely hopeless.'

'Why?' he asked. 'What do you mean? What's hopeless?'

'I mean, nothing can ever happen between us. Never *ever ever.*'

'What? What are you talking about? I don't even know what you mean.'

'I don't know why we're talking about this now,' said Barbara. 'I suppose it's because you're going away and that. Maybe you'll get hurt or shot or something. I don't know. But, the thing is, William, if you ever get to think about it, and I must admit I used to, all the time actually, when we were kids and that, and that night in my bed, I *still* think about it, but the thing is, well, we can't ever get married. No matter what, we just *can't.*'

Married!

Suddenly William felt nervous and breathless. He realized, for the first time, that all he *ever* wanted to do was marry Barbara. He hadn't thought about it lately, not so plainly, had taken it for granted, but now it was obvious. That's what all his longing was about: to *marry* Barbara.

He could hardly speak but he managed to ask the obvious:

'Why not?'

'Well, Mummy told me about it ages ago, and I've heard it from other people too.'

'What?' demanded William.

'We're cousins, William.'

'So?'

'Well, apparently, if cousins get married the chances are there'll be something wrong with their children.'

'Wrong? Like what?'

'They could be deformed or something. Cripples. Or mad even. Idiots. Loonies. Wouldn't that be awful?'

William had never heard such a thing. He didn't know what to think or say and so he said nothing. He was confused. On the one hand he was happy and excited to at last be talking to Barbara about how they both felt — about *love* — and to learn that she really did feel the same as he did. But, at the same time, now, with this news, he was disappointed and depressed.

'The thing is,' continued Barbara quickly, as if she were saying something she had long suppressed, 'it's even *more* than that.'

'Is it?' William wondered what more there could be to such news?

'Well, we're not ordinary cousins, are we?'

'Aren't we?'

'No. Definitely not.'

'Why? What are we then?'

'Our mothers aren't just ordinary sisters are they. They're twins, William. Identical twins.'

William nodded.

'And think about it: our fathers were brothers.'

William nodded again.

'So, don't you get it?' Barbara sounded and *was* frustrated, 'We're much more than ordinary cousins, William. Can't you see?'

'What are we then?' asked William again.

'I don't know,' said Barbara quickly, in frustration, 'I really don't. All I know is that if ordinary cousins shouldn't get married then double cousins like us — whatever we are, whatever it's called, I don't know — definitely shouldn't get married and have children. Definitely.'

'Oh,' said William.

William was twenty years old but for the rest of his life he never forgot the dread he felt at that moment on that day at the end of nineteen fifty-six.

Barbara noticed it at once. Standing in the door of the potting shed, and seeing what her well-meaning words had done to him, she immediately understood his disappointment. She understood because she too had experienced it. She secretly sympathized with him. But she didn't tell him that.

She longed to explain, but didn't, that she had tried to overcome her own disappointment by trying to enjoy a busy and exciting social life, with other men, which she realized must have been painful for him to see.

She wanted to apologize about that but didn't. But she vowed to herself then, at that moment, as she saw the pain on William's face, that if she couldn't marry *him*, her dear cousin, then she would marry no one. To marry anyone but him would be too hurtful. She knew that. And she didn't want to hurt him any more. Or ever again.

She didn't tell him that either.

From that day William involuntarily wrapped himself in a soft and comforting blanket of melancholia. The older and wiser of his friends assumed, not altogether wrongly, he was suffering from a secret and unrequited love. But Barbara knew better. She knew exactly what had happened. It hurt her deeply to see him so hurt. And yet she knew — without doubt — that the only cure for his permanent sorrow was a permanent impossibility.

One of the blokes in my barracks was rushed to hospital with peritonitis. We all thought it was a painful way to dodge parade.

This snippet of inconsequential news was typical of the trivial content of William's letters to Barbara during the three months of his military training.

Others similarly trivial included:

I had a bit of toothache. The army dentist said it had to come out. What a butcher. I bled like a stuck pig.

You ask how I'm coping with the drills, etc. Well I'm pretty fit really but I must admit my feet get d _ _ _ ed sore after a day of marching. But I'm not the only one. Some blokes get terrible blisters.

Yesterday we spent the day on the firing range. I was shooting big old 303s left over from the Boer war I reckon. We had to aim at targets shaped like men. Japs and Jerries I suppose. My aim was pretty good but I don't really enjoy being around guns and tanks and things. Still, I suppose that's what the army's all about. B _ _ _ _ y war, shooting and killing.

Only two weeks to go. I must admit I'm now thoroughly sick of it all. I'll be so glad to get back home, back to work and a normal life.

You'll be 21 soon. Older than me. (Ha ha!) Are you going to have a party?

Conspicuous by its intentional absence was any note of affection. William's salutations were limited to *Dear Barbara* or *Dear Cousin,* while his valediction was always simply: *Cheers, William.*

Barbara's letters were not much different in their opening — *Dear William* — although she was a little less formal with closings that varied: *Kind regards, your cousin Barbara,* or even, once, *Affectionately yours, Barbara.*

Barbara's "news" — the content of her short letters — was as trivial as William's although each little item was read by William as though it were truly important.

We've had to pay old Mr Chapman down the road to do the lawns and hedges. He seems to enjoy the work but chats too much about his bad back.

I've started going to the pictures every Thursday with the oldies like you used to do. It's all right but they usually like different flicks than me. But, amazing, last Thursday I talked them into seeing that new Elvis Presley picture called Love Me Tender. They were reluctant at first but in fact they loved it. Loved Elvis. Can you believe it. 45 years old and they love "Elvis the Pelvis". Can't stop talking about him.

Poor Mrs Collet died suddenly on Friday. We all went to the funeral yesterday for your sake, to represent you. Mr Collet looked dreadful. I wonder how he'll manage the petrol station without his wife? They said she was only 52. Not that old really.

We had a big power cut the other night. It was out all over Mt Eden and Roskill and Sandringham. We were cooking dinner so we just had bread and jam for tea. Made a cuppa on the primus. Just as well we had plenty of candles after last time.

Not doing anything for my 21ˢᵗ. Lot of fuss about nothing. What about you? I suppose I'll be able to go to the pub and vote in November. Everyone says to vote for Mr Nash but I haven't decided yet. I don't like that Mr Holyoake do you?

So cool and detached were the cousins' frequent correspondence for those three months that an outsider reading them, if that were possible, would naturally conclude that they were written under duress, out of duty rather than desire, although he would be puzzled why people so indifferent to each other should write so often.

Barbara and William too would have found it hard to explain the detached tone of their letters. It was as if knowing they would never consummate their mutual love they silently agreed to never express *any* show of affection. And so they were reduced to writing a lot about nothing while privately wishing they could express their true feelings about *everything*.

Meanwhile Barbara, having determined to marry no man if she couldn't marry William, decided there was no point in dating *any* man. Any form of fun which excluded William seemed meaningless.

William, without knowing Barbara's resolve to marry no one but him, assumed — even before he returned from his army training — that she would inevitably marry someone else. And so he mentally shrugged off the proverbial insulating blanket he had assumed as protection against further emotional pain and decided that, without Barbara, he might as well start leading, or trying to lead, a normal life.

There was, he thought, no alternative.

Chapter 8

Unlike other young men and women of their generation, Barbara and William preferred to let their twenty-first birthdays pass without acknowledgement. They both felt glum, for the same reason, seeing no reason to celebrate anything. Their mothers wanted to make some sort of fuss — perhaps a joint party with friends — not realizing that neither cousin had any special friends and, even if they did, neither was in the mood to celebrate their so-called "coming-of-age" when, amongst other freedoms granted by law, they would be able to marry without parental consent.

And so it was a pair of well-meaning but confused mothers who arranged a special dinner at home for each occasion during which the celebrant — Barbara first, William later — was presented with no more than a key-shaped mirror engraved on the front, in a swirling script, with the slogan "Happy 21st Birthday" and signed on the wooden back by the other three present.

At Barbara's intimate little dinner Mildred couldn't help making a pathetic and tearful little speech about how proud her Robert would be to see his darling little girl looking so grown up and so beautiful.

'I only hope, my darling,' she said, wiping her eyes with one hand while toasting her sherry glass with the other, 'that you find and marry a young man as handsome and loving as your wonderful father.'

It was a sad sentiment, uttered with the best of intentions, but it made William cringe and Barbara weep with misunderstood tears.

Six weeks later Millicent was unable to echo her sister's toast but did say, for William's sake, and in an effort to at least acknowledge her long-lost husband, how proud she was to be the mother of such a tall, handsome, kind, gentle, well-educated and hard-working young man. She was sure his father, wherever he was — 'the bastard,' she added acidly — would be equally proud.

'You must know, William,' she said in a belated attempt at charity, 'that your poor father couldn't help being the way he was. It was the war, you know. Everything he went through. It *must* have been.

'He was all right before that, wasn't he Millie,' she added. Looking to her sister for confirmation.

Mildred nodded grimly.

'I know, Mother,' said William kindly. 'And I know what you and Aunt Millie went through to bring us up, me and Barbara. We do appreciate it you know. Absolutely no complaints, eh Barbara?'

Barbara nodded and smiled while Millicent began to weep from a mixture of sadness for what might have been and pride in what was.

Once William had returned from military training he and Barbara continued to suppress their real feelings for each other, maintaining only what their mothers, any other acquaintance or casual observer, saw as a normal level of cousinly relations; evidently cordial but somewhat detached.

But to each of them it was a constant strain.

William resumed his work at the Farmers — he was welcomed back by colleagues who had missed his quiet but reliable presence — knowing he was in the last few months of his apprenticeship beyond which he would be a qualified printer entitled to work in any print shop in the country, in the world, for a tradesman's wage.

Meanwhile Barbara was still enjoying her work, being especially respected there, at Smith and Brown, for her elite position as a private secretary in the executive suite. Having foresworn marriage to anyone but William, she rarely went out during the weekend and instead diligently dedicated herself to housekeeping duties. It was a change which the self-absorbed William hardly noticed as he kept up his demanding gardening and house maintenance role.

William thought of buying a car, which he could easily afford, but he put it off knowing he would be obliged to offer Barbara a lift to work which she would have no reason to decline. The potential for awkwardness and constant emotional pain — for them both — was enough to keep him carless.

Eventually, inevitably, the strain of pretending to be no more than friends, while living together in the same house, sleeping in adjacent bedrooms, became too much for the cousins. Something had to give. They knew it, felt it, independently, without conferring.

Mildred and Millicent, glad and grateful to be living together in the familiar home of their shared childhood, which was now in their joint possession, innocently failed to register that the tension between Barbara and William, which they had never noticed anyway, had recently increased alarmingly. They naively assumed that nothing could or would spoil their own peaceful lives and that they and their children would somehow continue to live together in Brockley Cottage happily ever after.

It was William who finally broke the spell. It happened early in nineteen fifty-eight.

William knew that his apprenticeship was almost complete. That meant he'd be free to leave Farmers and start a new life somewhere, anywhere, where he wouldn't have to live with Barbara who, week by week, seemed to grow more beautiful, more desirable, and less accessible.

Out of sight, he decided, would be out of mind.

Leaving home, perhaps leaving Auckland, was something he dreaded while knowing it was absolutely necessary.

He set about buying a car.

The Farmers had helped him get his licence, so he could run errands and make deliveries. Drawing on the experience and knowledge gained at Collet's and since, he eventually chose a second-hand low-mileage 1950 Austin A40 being sold by a non-driving woman in Ellerslie who was left with the car when her husband died. It was an affordable and reliable model, easy to maintain, which he was sure would get him wherever he wanted to go for many years into the future.

Then, working quietly on his own, towards the day when he would be a qualified tradesman, he set about making arrangements that would surprise and shock the three women in his life all of whom he loved dearly, one above the others, none of whom he wished to hurt but one of whom he could no longer bear to be in constant nearness.

One day in March, having completed his apprenticeship, he was presented with his papers by Mr Tasker, the Farmers printing department manager, at a small after-work ceremony in the staff lunchroom. He didn't tell Mr Tasker then — it didn't seem appropriate — but the next day, a Friday, he resigned, much to the dismay of Mr Tasker and all his colleagues, young and old.

'So what's your plan, lad?' asked Mr Tasker. 'I do hope you're staying in the trade. You're a fine printer, you know. One of the best.'

'I'm going to New Plymouth,' said William. 'Got a job there no trouble at all.'

Mr Tasker was shocked. 'Not on one of the papers, surely?' he asked. Mr Tasker was contemptuous of daily newspapers. He admired *quality* printing, taking great pride in what his department produced.

'Oh, no,' said William. 'Medium-sized firm. Family business. Crosthwaite & Scott Limited. They've got a big letterpress department. New Heidelburgs. And plenty of work.'

'Never heard of them,' said Mr Tasker.

William shrugged. 'They're not huge or anything,' he said. 'But they're big in New Plymouth and Taranaki.'

'But why New Plymouth?' asked the older man with genuine curiosity.

'Need a fresh start away from Auckland, Mr Tasker,' said William with a regret that was obvious. 'I really do.'

'I see,' said William's kindly old manager, guessing there was a girl involved somewhere in William's decision. 'But, as I said, why New Plymouth?'

'Got an uncle there,' said William referring to the twins' older but estranged brother Charles. 'An aunt and cousins and that. They're going to help me get started.'

Millicent was truly shocked when William told her he was moving to New Plymouth.

'But where will you live?' she asked in horror.

'I'm staying with Uncle Charles and Aunt Ruby,' said William. 'They've got a big house in a place called Brooklands.'

'Never heard of it,' said Millicent dismissively.

Sixty-one-year-old Charles Duncan Brockley had long ago left Auckland to start a new life in New Plymouth away from his father whom he considered an eccentric irresponsible wastrel, a demanding and unloving husband, and a father who was unreasonably strict. There, married with children, he lost all emotional attachment to Brockley Cottage which he considered no better than a pile of rotting wood. He might have once expected to inherit the property but later had no objection when it passed to his young sisters.

He hardly knew the twins whom he thought to be spoiled, immature and somewhat "silly". He did know they had grown up and married local brothers, and had a child each, a girl and a boy about the same age, a niece and a nephew for him and his wife, young cousins for his own children. He was also aware that one of the twin's husbands was killed in the war while the other man, alive but utterly delinquent, had altogether abandoned his wife and child.

Thus did the twins earn the remote sympathy if not the love of their older brother who had welcomed the approach of one of their children, his nephew, William Conwyne.

'But you don't know Charles and Ruby,' protested Millicent. 'I hardly know them myself,' she added.

'I met them once, at a funeral somewhere,' said William. 'Years ago.'

'What funeral?'

'I don't know,' said William. 'Someone. A relative I suppose. I was only young. You took me. You and Aunt Mildred. Barbara, too.'

'I don't remember that, sweet boy,' said Millicent with a dismissive, condescending wave. 'You're making it up.'

'No I'm not,' insisted William. 'I met them. Uncle Charles and Aunt Ruby. So when I got the job in New Plymouth I wrote to them and they said I can stay with them until I find something for myself.'

Mildred and Barbara were equally shocked — Barbara especially so — when, later that night, while William was out familiarizing himself with his new car, Millicent told them about William's plans.

'Oh, you poor thing,' said Mildred sympathetically, knowing how she would feel if Barbara left Auckland to live so far away.

Barbara, though, said nothing then but went up to bed early and cried softly in the privacy of her bedroom. She longed to talk to William, to hold him and kiss him and beg him not to go. She slept poorly and stayed in bed for the entire weekend because she felt so wretched, thought she must look wretched, and simply didn't want William to see her looking so blotchy-faced, red-eyed and miserable.

Her mother and aunt — but not William — assumed that Barbara was ill when, the following Saturday morning, she stayed in bed rather than stand on the veranda with them as they waved a sad, tearful, goodbye to their son and nephew, her beloved cousin, William.

Chapter 9

By the end of that year William was settled into his job with Crosthwaite & Scott in New Plymouth. He was an excellent and conscientiousness tradesman who quickly earned the respect of his supervisors and colleagues for that as well as for his genial nature. He made friends easily at work as well as at the tennis club, near the Brockley home in Brooklands, which he joined not long after arriving.

All his new friends, whether workmates, tennis players or others, were men. Although there were a few young women in the office and tennis club, who naturally found the "new chap from Auckland" to be both "dishy" and eligible, William — who missed Barbara terribly but was determined to get on with his life — was oblivious to them and their flirting.

He was living with his uncle and aunt who enjoyed his young and agreeable company and made it clear he was welcome to stay. As a result he came to know his older New Plymouth cousins, Betty and Cedric, their spouses and children.

For the first time in his life William felt part of a real family.

Barbara and William wrote regularly but they each withheld any written show of affection just as they had when William was away in the army. They concentrated on purely routine news and matters.

There was, however, one theme to Barbara's news: that the house and garden missed William's constant care and attention and that the three women were now reluctantly contributing equally to a fund from which they paid "a man" to take regular care of the lawns and gardens, and paid other tradesmen for necessary household repairs and maintenance when required. But, they said, no one was as efficient and caring of Brockley Cottage as he.

William's letters, too, contained a consistent theme, an element which he unconsciously repeated but which unintentionally caused a mild jealousy in Barbara and resentment in the twin mothers. Rather than write of his work and his colleagues — both of which were central to his new life but which he assumed would not interest his correspondents — he wrote instead of his growing closeness to his New Plymouth family, a closeness which the twin mothers, Charles's "baby sisters in Auckland", had never, in their insular twinship, experienced.

And Barbara, locked into the life of Brockley Cottage, and the twins' unique intimacy, since infancy, had never met nor wanted to meet any of her New Plymouth relatives. She now resented them only because William was obviously fond of them and they of him.

Thus the love and longing Barbara and William still had for each other, even at a distance, remained unwritten just as it had for so long been unspoken; their birthday cards to each other being the only exception.

Dear Cousin, wrote William ahead of the neutral-sounding verse in the birthday card he posted to Barbara in July for her twenty-second birthday; he signed it *Regards, William.*

Dear William, wrote Barbara in her card to William at the beginning of September. She wanted to write 'My Darling William' but didn't although she did sign it *Your affectionate cousin, Barbara,* to which she added *X X X.*

Christmas nineteen fifty-eight marked a quiet but significant marker in William's relationship with his Auckland family.

Since he had moved to New Plymouth the three women in his life had unthinkingly and selfishly assumed that his absence was temporary; that before long he would of course come back to Brockley Cottage, where he belonged, and take charge, once again, of the house and garden maintenance; that they would no longer have to tolerate the comings and goings of various gardeners and tradesmen; that life for them — for the four of them — would return to "normal".

They were surprised and disappointed, therefore, to learn that William wouldn't be coming home for Christmas.

The news came first to Millicent, as it was her "turn" to receive a William letter, and confirmed to Barbara in a Christmas card. Millicent was bitterly disappointed; since William's birth she had never celebrated Christmas, nor the Boxing Day birthday she shared with Mildred, without him. Mildred was puzzled by the news and surprised by her nephew's independent spirit. Like Millicent she had assumed that William's move to New Plymouth was a youthful "phase", an aberration, and that he would naturally, inevitably, eventually, return to Brockley Cottage where he belonged.

Barbara, though, was utterly, terribly, shocked by the news. She had planned at Christmas to break the ice, as it were, with William; to show her feelings towards him — her deep affection — openly, and to encourage him to do the same. She made her decision when she learned, from an older woman at work who knew about such things, that there was no *legal* reason to stop cousins from marrying each other. Furthermore, there wasn't even anything in law to stop cousins having children together; it was merely considered medically "unwise" and "risky" particularly — especially — for closer-than-normal cousins like her and William.

Barbara's hope for Christmas, therefore, was that she and William could again become at least as close and loving as they had been as children. Her *secret* hope was that he could see and agree that they might — actually *could* — get married provided they were careful and didn't have children. And she dreamed that, having agreed, he would take her in his arms and they would kiss and, after years of longing, she would thrill to feel his body close to hers.

Meanwhile, in New Plymouth, William had learned, from living with his uncle's close and loving family, how much women liked to be mothers, and how motherhood suited them. He had come to the conclusion, therefore, that Barbara would almost certainly, naturally, *want* to have children. Accordingly, he reasoned, as she was afraid of having children with him she should feel free to marry someone — not him — with whom having children would be safe.

And so, before Barbara had the chance to explain herself — that she would willingly forego motherhood if he could forego fatherhood — William decided it would be unfair to expect her to not have children merely for his sake.

As Christmas approached neither of the confused cousins knew of the other's thoughts and decisions. As it turned out, though, William had little time to think of anything as, for the first time in his life, he experienced a real New Zealand family Christmas.

Although he had met his older cousins Betty and Cedric separately, dinner on Christmas day was the first time he had seen the New Plymouth Brockley family together. Cedric, who despite being eighteen years William's senior was to become a good friend, was married to Pat; they had a teenage son. Betty and her husband George Morse had two teenage children; they had all travelled across from their home in Hamilton. And so there were ten of them at the table for Christmas dinner. It wasn't an especially big party but it was an entirely new Christmas experience for William.

Charles and Ruby weren't especially religious but they did start important meals — and what could be more important than a family Christmas dinner? — with grace, led by Charles who mentioned and welcomed William. Of course there were Christmas crackers — with colourful paper hats, silly toys and puerile jokes — and lively discussions about the merits of the presents given and received.

The meal was a traditional Christmas menu utterly familiar to all present, to all New Zealanders, except William. There, at that table, on that special day, he discovered the delights of stuffed chicken — there were two of them — ceremoniously brought to the table by his aunt where it was carefully carved and served by his Uncle Charles. Then he shared in the delight of a flaming Christmas pudding in which were concealed numerous silver coins and upon which was spread brandy-butter sauce. Above all, though, he discovered the intoxicating joy of sharing a special occasion with a proper family, united by love, and led by a strong and caring father.

For William it was a bitter-sweet experience. Much as he enjoyed it he couldn't help wishing that Barbara could have been there to see and experience what he had seen and experienced that happy but poignant Christmas day.

Meanwhile in Auckland Barbara had a quiet Christmas day with her mother and aunt, celebrated with a simple meal and a glass of sweet sherry. The twin mothers' birthday the next day passed without celebration at all.

Life passed uneventfully, not unpleasantly but separately, for Barbara and William over the next few years although they both knew that life would be exceedingly *more* pleasant in the other's company. But by then they were each resigned to not marrying the other although their views of an alternative future differed markedly.

Barbara continued to be happy in her Smith and Brown job while Smith and Brown continued to be happy with her. Indeed she was highly respected by everyone there. She even came to meet some of the firm's most important customers — inevitably wealthy women of middle- to advanced-age — who befriended her as if she were as educated, wealthy, married and well-connected as they.

As a result of mixing with the upper echelon of Auckland's furniture-buying society she received many invitations — to the pictures, dances and parties — from some of the city's most eligible and attractive young men. However, she socialized only lightly without making any commitment concerning the future which she was determined to face alone.

She realized, though — if not fully appreciated at her tender age — the enduring implications of her decision to marry no one but William: that she would eventually, inevitably, become an old, childless and lonely spinster. It was not a thought she enjoyed — she generally managed to put out of her mind — but the alternative thought horrified her: to marry an unmet man whom she didn't love, and to have his children, merely to conform to society's expectations and so avoid loneliness.

There was also a melodramatic martyrdom to her decision: the idea of being loyal and faithful to a secret lover who never would or could return her devotion, and to thereby appear mysteriously sad to others who would have to admire her stoicism. It was an immature concept, forgivable at her age, which she soon abandoned. But she never abandoned or regretted her decision to remain faithful to the only man she could ever love.

William, though, had decided that pining for the impossible was futile; he *had* to get on with life. And so he consciously shrugged off the melancholia, which had become a bad habit, and returned, easily, to the happy blend of being earnest when necessary but cheerful whenever possible, which is how he was seen by his New Plymouth family, colleagues, and all who met him thereafter.

He was, after all, only twenty-two when he moved to New Plymouth where he had found a new family and a new way of life. He had been thoroughly embraced by the Brockley family; not only his Uncle Charles and Aunt Ruby but also by their children and grand-children. Indeed, he quickly came to know more of his mother and aunt's family than they did — or cared to — and could see and appreciate what they had missed and were still missing by their stubborn Auckland-based twinship. It was an insularity which they seem to have passed on to Barbara who, William judged from her letters, seemed to care little for the New Plymouth Brockleys.

Although William's newly-met uncle and aunt knew and remembered Mildred and Millicent in Auckland, their children and grandchildren didn't. And although they were all vaguely aware of

Barbara's existence, she was rarely mentioned by William and never referred to by the rest of the family. As a result William found it easy to park her memory where he could find it, privately, if and when required.

Unlike Barbara, he enjoyed a busy social life, finding no shortage of young New Plymouth women his age — or even older — willing to date such a handsome and pleasant young man with a steady job and a nice car. But while he was enjoying life so much, being flattered by the female attention he attracted, he met no one who interested him even slightly beyond friendship. Nevertheless, and also unlike Barbara, he had not ruled out the possibility of a future romance; unlike her, he saw no merit in a romantic martyrdom. Resigned to the idea that he and Barbara would never be more than friendly cousins, with shared and pleasant memories, he hoped — perhaps subconsciously — that marriage and fatherhood might be possible if he should meet just the "right" girl.

Chapter 10

Gradually, over the next few years, letter writing between the cousins, as well as between William and his mother, became less frequent; it occurred to all parties that there was little in their lives that would be interesting or newsworthy to others.

Millicent had come to accept that William might never return which meant that she and Mildred, and Barbara too, would have to make permanent arrangements for the care of Brockley Cottage which, in its dilapidated old age, demanded constant maintenance. They were also, slowly, losing control over the house's park-like demesne learning in the process that tradesmen and nurserymen, despite their qualifications, testimonials and earnest efforts, are no substitute for a man emotionally connected and committed to the property as their otherwise lazy father was for so long followed by young William for a period too short.

Barbara, who never revealed her love of William to the twin mothers, continued to suppress the enduring sadness she felt at his permanent absence. When doing anything at home, alone, in the house or garden, she imagined William was at her side. She sometimes — often — visited the gloomy potting shed to find William's pots and tools, even his leather gardening gloves and apron, just as he had left them. Only, at each visit, they were covered in a little more dust.

'Oh, dear William,' she often said aloud, with a sigh, 'I miss you so much.'

Despite William's occasional letters, cheery and newsy — or perhaps because of them, because they contained no hint of homesickness or regret — she couldn't help wondering, jealously, what he *wasn't* telling her. Surely, she thought, there were girls in his life as well as the men at his work and tennis club, and others he mentioned who evidently took him fishing, sailing, and hiking up Mount Egmont.

But, no. Only men friends were ever mentioned.

Barbara bore her sadness bravely; so well that her mother and aunt, who lived in total sympathy with *each other's* feelings, failed to notice the dimming of her once bright personality.

Eventually, inevitably, correspondence between New Plymouth and Mount Eden was reduced to cards at Christmas and birthdays which for Mildred and Millicent were only a day apart.

Once, though, in the middle of nineteen sixty, in an attempt to inject some "real" news into a letter to his mother, William mentioned in a postscript — merely an afterthought — a new New Plymouth girlfriend called Shirley Bateman who worked at McKenzies. It was a piece of trivial news to him in a letter which contained nothing else of consequence. He thought it might titillate his mother, which it did, causing her giggle girlishly with amusement as she read that passage to Mildred and Barbara.

'Oh, that *is* a surprise,' said Millicent when she came to the P.S. 'Isn't that nice.'

'It had to happen, I suppose,' said Mildred.

'I wonder what she's like,' said Millicent. She dropped her letter-holding hand to her lap and looked at the ceiling dreamily. 'I might have a daughter-in-law, Millie. Grandchildren even. Imagine it. Me, a grandmother.'

'Don't see me ever being a grandmother,' said Mildred. 'Not with Barbara.'

She turned then to address her daughter. But Barbara, deeply hurt, wasn't there.

'I don't know what's wrong with that girl lately, Millie,' Mildred said to her sister. 'I really don't.'

It was almost lunchtime on a Saturday morning when the post arrived. The three women stopped what they were doing — sharing the Saturday housekeeping chores — to set aside their cleaning cloths and feather dusters, and sit down together at the big dining table to read William's letter. Barbara had listened more from duty or habit than interest. She knew in advance that William's news would be neither new nor interesting. She was shocked, therefore, when her aunt read out the few lines at the end about a girl called Shirley Bateman. And she was somewhat perplexed when she saw that William's mother seemed pleased when she looked meaningfully across the table at her sister.

Barbara stood up then and, head down, fast-walked into the parlour where she shut the door, sat on a chair beside the fireplace, bent forward and began to cry.

When the worst of her sobbing was over she sat back, bent back her head, and looked up at the ceiling through wetted eyes.

'Oh, darling William,' is all she said aloud but quietly.

She actually *wanted* to shout: 'I love you, William Conwyne, with all my heart. I really do. I wish you were here. I wish you'd never ever gone to New Plymouth. I *hate* that place. And I *hate* Shirley Bateman whoever she is.'

A young man called for Barbara that evening but she refused to come down from her room. Mildred had to turn him away with apologies and the excuse that she was ill.

'Such a nice young chap,' she said to her sister. 'And you should have seen his car.'

'Is she *really* sick?' asked Millicent. "What's wrong with her?'

'I don't know, said a frustrated Mildred. 'She's really been acting quite strange lately.'

Barbara did leave her room that night but only to use the toilet and have a bath. She had no tea that night. Nor did she get up for breakfast the next morning.

'There's tea and toast on a tray down here,' her mother called up the grand staircase, but it was still there, untouched, later in the day.

Only when the twins left for work on the Monday morning did a tired, hungry, red-eyed, blotchy-faced and thoroughly miserable Barbara leave her room to bathe and eat and ring Smith and Brown to excuse her absence from work due, she said, to a flu which she didn't want to spread around the office.

Millicent replied warmly to William's letter saying she was sure Shirley must be a nice girl — *even if she works at McKenzies* — and that *we all look forward to meeting her one day soon*. She went on to suggest — hope — that he might bring Shirley home for Christmas before adding a P.S. *You might not hear from Barbara for a while as she hasn't been very well.*

She got a fright a few evenings later when she answered the phone to hear William's familiar voice. The twins had never received or made a toll call.

'Oh, my darling boy,' she said loudly, almost shouting, although the line was perfectly clear. 'Is something wrong? Has something happened?'

William was relieved that Barbara hadn't answered.

'No, Mother,' he said. 'Nothing like that.'

'Well, what on earth is it? Is everything all right there? Is Charles all right? And Ruby?'

'Mother,' insisted William. 'It's nothing like that.'

'Well what is it then, darling? Why are you ringing your mother like this? It must be jolly expensive.'

'Don't worry about that, Mother. I was worried about Barbara. Is she all right? What exactly's wrong with her?'

'Oh, *Barbara*,' said Millicent dismissively. 'She's all right, silly girl.'

'She's not a girl, Mother,' said William, somewhat offended for Barbara's sake. 'So is she all right?'

'She's all right. A bit run down that's all. Do you want to speak to her?'

William would love to have spoken to Barbara, especially to reassure himself that she was well, but the idea butterflied his stomach.

'No, no,' he replied quickly. 'It's all right. Don't bother her. As long as she's all right, that's the main thing.'

'I'm all right too,' said Millicent sarcastically. 'And so's your Aunt Millie.'

'That's good, Mother,' said William who wasn't listening. He was beginning to consider the cost of the call. 'I better go.'

Despite Millicent's casual indifference to Barbara's health, at least at that time, in the beginning — telling William she was just a "silly girl" — Barbara was not merely "a bit run down" but *was* undeniably ill.

However, both the cause and nature of her illness were impossible to determine.

After hearing William's news about Shirley Bateman on that Saturday morning in August, nineteen sixty, Barbara went to her bed for a full week saying only that she didn't feel right. "Queer in the head" was the vague term she used.

She returned to work the following week, looking pale but otherwise well, but lasted only a day. The next day, after lunch, she was sent home by taxi, at the firm's expense, when, for no apparent reason, she began to cry at her desk staining the letter she was holding, having just finished typing it, ready for Mr Simmonite's signature.

Over the next few weeks her anxious mother and aunt did their best to care for her, often taking turns, when they could, to stay home. Eventually, though, the twins' supervisor at The Farmers began to complain about their frequent absences.

Alone at home all day, not eating or drinking properly, not exercising, Barbara became more ill. She lost weight and muscle tone and so, frail and weak, was unable to return to work. Doctor East, the twins' old doctor, and his young and more-recently qualified partner, could at first offer no explanation or therapy for their patient's condition. They could recommend only that she eat nourishing food, in small easily-digested amounts but often, drink plenty of fluids, be kept warm, and sheltered from stress.

When, despite exhaustive tests, tonics and medications, Barbara's health neither improved nor worsened the doctors confided in the twins that they believed her illness was not due to a physical disease but was a psychological escape from something she found unpleasant or even frightening.

'She must have received some sort of shock,' said Doctor East. 'Have you any idea what that might have been?'

The twins were mystified.

'Well, it's not a medical term we like,' said the doctor, 'but most people understand "nervous breakdown" well enough.'

'Is that what you think?' asked Mildred.

The old doctor nodded soberly. 'There's nothing physically wrong with the lass,' he said. 'We know that for sure.'

'So what must we do?' asked a worried and frightened Mildred. 'Will she get well again? It's such a worry.'

'I'm sure she'll be fine,' said the doctor. 'She'll rally in her own time. The mind, you know—' he lightly tapped his left temple '— a mysterious thing. The poor wee lass just needs time. We have consulted specialists, as you know. They all concur. She needs time and your loving care.'

Time passed.

The directors of Smith and Brown were both worried and vexed by Barbara Conwyne's continued absence. Eventually after three months they were compelled to write to her, over the managing director's signature, in the most formal terms.

After due consideration, they wrote, *the directors have reluctantly concluded that the firm can no longer afford nor accept your permanent absence. An experienced lady from the secretarial pool has therefore been appointed to fill your position in the executive suite. Accordingly, as of this date, you should no longer consider herself an employee of Smith and Brown Limited.*

Should your health be restored you would be welcomed back to the firm, providing a suitable position is available; alternatively the writer would be pleased to furnish a testimonial properly reflecting the esteem with which you were held while here at Smith and Brown where you proved to be a consistently pleasant, honest, diligent and reliable employee whom we would have no hesitation in recommending to any potential employer.

Reassured by his mother about Barbara's health, William continued to enjoy a busy work and social life in New Plymouth. He especially appreciated being part of his uncle and aunt's family realizing that they really were *his* relatives, *his* family. And being included in their friends and family celebrations, sharing their achievements and disappointments, birthdays and anniversaries, he understood, at last, the value of the family life he had missed.

He also came to understand that his mother and aunt had never *needed* the rest of their family; that their familial needs had always been met, since infancy and still, by each other. It's not that they disliked their New Plymouth family, they simply had no need of them. They had no need of anyone but each other.

Only away from Brockley Cottage could he see that the twin mothers' relationship was singularly strange, probably unhealthy. But as they had always been the same he assumed they would never change.

He might have resented his strange upbringing, being deprived of what other children considered a normal family life, but, rather, he felt sorry for his mother and aunt, and Barbara too who, he could see, was stuck in Brockley Cottage with two oddly unconventional middle-aged women who had little interest in the world beyond themselves, each other, their absurdly named "cottage" in Mount Eden, and their work at The Farmers in Hobson Street.

He worried about Barbara, fearing that without becoming part of the Brockley family as he had, and so seeing more of the world, she would grow isolated and lonely, as odd as her mother and aunt. A sad prospect for someone he still thought was beautiful, loving and lovable, the only woman he would happily marry if only it were possible.

Chapter 11

Alas, William would have been more worried about Barbara if he had known how weak, frail, pale and deeply sad she really was; how she was hardly able to raise herself from the bed where she had been confined since hearing his brief and innocent allusion to a girl called Shirley Bateman.

Barbara, meanwhile, had no idea that Shirley Bateman meant *nothing* to William; that he had long ago abandoned her for a flashy blonde called Queeny McQuinlan who was followed by Vonny Shellford, Glenda Magill, Sheila Corbett and many more equally attractive young women all drawn to the tall, dark, young and handsome William Conwyne and his almost-new Mark II Zephyr. Shirley Bateman forgotten, William thought none of those who followed worthy of inclusion in the occasional letter of trivial news to his mother or Barbara.

But Barbara didn't know that, and so, obsessed by the thought of the notorious Shirley Bateman, her unhealthy fretting continued.

While still pale, and feeling weak, Barbara was somewhat better when William arrived to spend Christmas in Auckland. Christmas day was on a Sunday that year; he drove up from New Plymouth on the Saturday and spent the weekend and the holiday Monday at Brockley Cottage, returning to New Plymouth on the Tuesday.

The Christmas dinner fare at Brockley Cottage was familiar to William and although he enjoyed it, and said so, he couldn't help comparing it to the New Plymouth Brockley family's lavish

Christmas dinner of a year earlier which was preceded by their raucous gift-giving ritual. But in the Brockley Cottage manner, well-remembered by William, simple and inexpensive Christmas gifts were exchanged in the morning, without fuss or ceremony, William's being the only ones not purchased at Farmers and not wrapped in Farmers Christmas paper. And at lunch there were no crackers and no silly hats, and no laughing and joking before or during the roast chicken lunch, and no flaming Christmas pudding stuffed with coins.

Nevertheless, William enjoyed himself immensely especially as he sat opposite Barbara where, from across the great breadth of the ancient dining table, he could see her every expression, and show by his, he hoped, how much he loved and missed her. He hardly noticed how thin and wan she was, perhaps because love is blind, perhaps because Barbara was making a special effort to be good company. Perhaps it was a little of both.

The next evening, the evening of Boxing Day, William was also there to celebrate the twins' forty-eighth birthday dinner at which the same four people — no others were invited — celebrated quietly while consuming a glass of *Riesling* and the Christmas dinner left-overs.

Once again he sat opposite Barbara and hoped, wishfully perhaps, that she enjoyed the view across the table as much as he did.

Until that Christmas visit William had thought he was managing well in New Plymouth without Barbara. He imagined he was gradually thinking of her less often, and with less longing, being happy with his New Plymouth family, being busy in his new job, joining new clubs and meeting new friends. He was surprised, therefore, by how glad he was — *really* glad — to see her again. He thought she looked thinner somehow, pale and somewhat pensive and detached. But the loving feelings for her, which he had denied for so long, came rushing back which made him both glad and sad.

Nevertheless, after so many months away, denying his feelings, he now didn't hesitate to hug her to him — gently, as she felt more slender and delicate than he remembered — and bend down to kiss her tenderly on the forehead. Barbara, for her part, surrendered utterly to his hold, turning her head to lay it against his chest.

Resting there it took all her inner strength not to tearfully collapse in his arms. She didn't. But she couldn't control her silent voice which cried out and echoed around inside her head: 'Oh, William, my darling, cousin, I love you with all my heart. I always will. But you have a new life. I know that now. So now that I'm well again I really must get on with mine.'

Neither Doctor East nor his partner could explain Barbara's return to wellness. They said only that it confirmed their belief — and the belief of the specialists they had consulted — that her illness had had a psychological cause, a form of hysteria not unknown in emotional young women, and that its sudden departure meant that the original cause — deeply felt and perhaps hidden even from the patient herself — was no longer present.

Barbara, though, knew exactly what had happened. In the three weeks before Christmas, when William was planning his trip to Auckland, looking forward to giving his powerful new car an outing on the open road, Millicent asked, in a letter, whether they would at last have the pleasure of meeting his girlfriend, Shirly Bateman.

William replied — with what amounted, in writing, to a dismissive, almost hilarious, laugh — that he hadn't seen Shirley Bateman for ages, that she was nothing to him, and that there was absolutely no steady girlfriend in his life. None. He would be coming on his own.

That news, shared with Mildred and Barbara, as the twins sat in Barbara's sickroom one evening at the beginning of the month, triggered an abrupt emotional change in Barbara which led to her complete physical recovery. She realized, clearly and consciously, admitting it to herself, for the first time, that she had been foolish to have been jealously hurt by William's news of having a girlfriend. Obviously, she thought, being so tall, handsome, well-dressed, kind and considerate, with a good job, good prospects, and a nice car, any girl would be stupid not to see what a wonderful catch he was. And as much as she wished he lived in Auckland — not necessarily at Brockley Cottage but somewhere nearby — she knew, from his once-frequent but now occasional letters, that he enjoyed being part of a big family which he could never have with her in Auckland.

Inevitably, and quickly then, Barbara resigned herself to the certain knowledge that William would eventually, sooner or later, marry a beautiful girl, probably in New Plymouth, where he would buy a house and settle down to have children, raise a family and so lead the sort of ideal life which she guessed he longed for and which she knew would never be hers. She decided then, with his Christmas visit pending, that it was better, for her own sake, her health and welfare, to accept the inevitable and wish William nothing but a happy life.

In doing so she became resigned to her *own* future. True to her secret promise, to marry no man if she couldn't marry William, she decided that, as a single woman, unmarried, unloved and childless, she would love and support William for the rest of their lives until they were inevitably, one day, parted by death. 'Till death us do part, William,' was her silent and secret vow.

Thus was she so much better, in mind and body, when William spent that Christmas weekend of nineteen sixty with her in his old home.

William enjoyed his short stay at Brockley Cottage but not enough to stay beyond the holiday weekend. Seeing Barbara again, and spending time alone with her, was a sort of painful joy. Twice they went driving in his new Zephyr; once on the long and scenic drive to Piha, stopping at Titirangi for a milkshake, and, on the morning before he left, around the waterfront to Saint Heliers Bay.

The weather was fine and hot that day so Barbara wore a flimsy sun-frock which, in William's eyes, made her look more beautiful than ever despite her unfamiliar thinness.

When they were alone together, on those drives, they talked and laughed continuously. Barbara at last wanted to know about William's life in New Plymouth, more especially about the members of the Brockley family of whom she knew nothing but a few faceless names.

She also asked about his army commitments. Didn't he have to go to camp or something for a few weeks every year? William said he received the notices from the army, which his mother had forwarded to New Plymouth, but he ignored them and nothing happened.

'They don't know where I live any more,' he said, 'and Mother's not telling them. And, anyway,' he added, 'no one but a few old warmongers really cares about CMT any more. That's what the blokes at work said, Uncle Charles too, and they're right.'

Barbara was a little surprised by William's rebellious attitude to authority. She thought it was quite unlike the compliant and conservative William she grew up with, and she was again intrigued by the big changes in his character wrought by a small change of address.

She could tell that the people he worked with — at Crosthwaite & Scott, she'd made a point of remembering the name — were important to him so she probed him about them. She was genuinely interested but hardly dared ask about his social life. Nevertheless William talked loosely about the tennis club, "the gang", and his "mates", and what they did together. He never mentioned any girls but Barbara guessed there must be *some* in "the gang".

In the end she was harmlessly envious of William's New Plymouth life; not only of the unmentioned girls, his family and friends, but that he was active in the tennis club and had learned to tramp and fish and sail and even play golf. Except for tennis, which he had always liked, they were activities in which he had never shown interest when they were young together, and of which she still knew nothing.

William wanted to know about Barbara's illness. He acknowledged that she had lost weight but said that she otherwise looked well enough. He wanted to say that she looked as beautiful as ever but he said only that he hoped she would soon be completely well.

In fact, though, he never learned how sick Barbara *really* was for those few months — Barbara didn't tell him and neither, at her behest, did the twin mothers — and so he didn't understand why, at least according to her, she had *resigned* from Smith and Brown. Barbara said only that she was sick of both how she had to be always so smartly and expensively dressed, for her "posh" employers and important customers, and getting the bus to and from Symonds Street every day.

'I'm going to find a new job in the new year,' she said. 'Something easy and near home.'

William had mixed feelings about his mother and aunt, not having seen them for three years. He thought, having just turned forty-eight, they were beginning to look and act *older* than other women their age. And he still couldn't understand why they cared nothing for their New Plymouth family. On the contrary, they seemed to resent them.

He also recognized something he'd never understood as a child: that despite their upbringing by a meek and indulgent mother and an irresponsible, snobby, unpleasant and profligate father who had quickly exhausted the considerable Brockley fortune, they had managed to get well-paid work together and so raise him and Barbara and somehow maintain the inherited and ridiculously large family home.

He also thought — with a concern he wished he could ignore — that, like its twin owners, Brockley Cottage, together with its outbuildings and gardens, was beginning to show its age. Inside, nothing had been changed since his grandfather's death in nineteen forty-five. The twins said they didn't *want* anything to change; they'd bought a new wireless and a refrigerator but refused to replace any furniture; they said they couldn't afford it. As a result they were living in a virtual museum of pre-war domestic life.

Outside, the stables, and the potting shed where he had once spent time doing nothing merely to avoid Barbara, were draped in uncontrolled ivy on one side and a venerable but untamed grape vine on the other, while those glass panes of the ancient greenhouse not cracked, broken or missing, were green with slimy moss.

The paint of the big house was dull, powdery, and flaking in parts. The wide front steps were showing signs of rot as were many of the floorboards on the verandas of both floors, the tin roof was showing rust in places and was otherwise spotted with dull and rough silvery-green and spreading lichen. Altogether, when seen from the street which it dominated, William thought the old house looked like a once-elegant old dowager, past her prime, standing wearily, a little hunched and bent, wearing shabby green robes from a bygone age, blissfully unaware of how she was seen by the modern world.

As he left Mount Eden on the Tuesday afternoon after Christmas, having said his goodbye to his mother and aunt indoors, before embracing Barbara gently on the rickety veranda — an embrace which Barbara freely returned — William paused, standing at the open door of his car, on the drive, to take a long and poignant look up at old Brockley Cottage, not knowing when next he might see and visit it and its three lady residents.

Chapter 12

The Farmers tea rooms were always especially busy during the summer school holidays. So once William returned to New Plymouth the twin mothers returned to work leaving the no-longer ill Barbara at home alone all day.

Suddenly, in the lovely hot summer of that new year, with the grounds of Brockley Cottage looking so fresh and green and lush, but overgrown, Barbara sat quietly, in the shade of the gazebo which William had swept out for her, surrounded by heavily-scented rose bushes, watching the noisy squabbling tuis clucking and knocking woodily somewhere unseen in the trees, and the piwakawaka frantically swooping and diving around the trees and bushes like little fighting aeroplanes. On the clipped and thirsty lawns the nervous little sparrows sought out the dry but nourishing seeds left by the lawnmower, while, beside and amongst them, the carnivorous blackbirds and thrushes probed and ruthlessly dragged out their shiny, stretched and reluctant worms. There, while watching and listening to the world around her, Barbara quietly rejoiced at her renewed good health, grateful that she had time to sit quietly, on her own, to appreciate and renew her love for the great estate founded by her great-grandfather.

She now couldn't understand how she could have lain in bed all day, week after week, for almost three months, usually with the curtains drawn, shutting out the broad and lovely garden far below, without feeling utterly bored.

She still thought often of William but now the thoughts were pleasant and generous, hoping, sincerely, that he had returned safely to New Plymouth and was enjoying what she hoped was a summer as pleasant for him there as it was for her in Auckland. Refreshingly absent were any anxious feelings of envy or longing. It was as though she were a new person, unrelated to the sad and frequently morose and pessimistic Barbara Conwyne she once was and had lately come to dislike.

Relieved to feel better about herself, her life and her future, she was determined to get a new job. One that would, she hoped, be close to home, be interesting but not too demanding. She knew she'd have to wait until most businesses restarted in the middle of January. Until then she began tidying up the long-neglected garden around her.

The work — trimming shrubs and trees and cutting back the boundary hedges — tired her at first but helped improve her strength, stamina and colour. She was soon able to work outside almost all day, under the summer sun until, during the week at least, it was time to prepare dinner for the home-coming twins.

It was while she was preparing tea one evening, early in February, scanning the Situations Vacant section of the *Star* while waiting for the potatoes to cook, that she saw an advertisement for what was called a "Girl Friday". The title was new to her but the brief job description caused her slap the kitchen table with the flat of her hand and announce, in a shout that echoed through the many rooms and two floors of the empty and otherwise hushed house:

'Perfect!'

As soon as she pulled open the heavy door of the factory Barbara was overwhelmed by the signature smell of a print shop. It was a combination of ink, turpentine and thinners, oil, electricity and warm paper which immediately and pleasantly evoked the presence of William, especially the pungent smell of the overalls he used to take home Friday nights to be washed on the weekend. That she was entering a workplace that would be familiar to William made her smile even before the big door swung closed behind her.

Hervey-Harrison was a well-established and somewhat old-fashioned commercial printing firm in Burleigh Street, only a short bus ride along Mount Eden Road from the Brockley Street bus stop. The plain single-storey concrete building was utterly without architectural merit. There was a dark and dirty cart dock at the Mount Eden Road end while the main entrance, through which Barbara made her entry, with a name sign above it, was up the hill, towards Khyber Pass, at the very middle of the long building.

Inside, Barbara found herself in a small lino-floored reception lobby, lined with framed print samples, where a girl — she seemed very young even to young Barbara — said that Mr Blackie was expecting her. She was then ushered into an office behind reception where sat, and then stood, Denzil Blackie, the managing director, whom she naturally addressed — then and always — as Mr Blackie.

Mr Blackie's office faced into the middle of what looked to Barbara, at a glance, like a vast, dark and dirty industrial nightmare of a space which seemed to have no limit to the right, left or ahead. It housed mysterious and ugly-looking machines, large and small, variously coloured black, navy blue, pale green and battleship grey, arranged, as far as she could tell, in no particular order or alignment. The office was double-glazed at the front allowing Mr Blackie to freely survey the activities of the factory floor. Despite the soundproofing, Barbara had to concentrate to hear Mr Blackie's questions, and even her own replies, over the constant and rhythmic rattling, whirring, grinding, clicking and hissing of the printing machines, and the occasional shouted conversations between the overalled machinists, coming from behind her as she sat facing Mr Blackie at his desk.

Barbara thought she performed poorly at the interview.

She wasn't nervous but she was a little confused; the noisy and messy Hervey-Harrison factory was nothing like the quiet Smith and Brown carpeted showroom, Mr Blackie's messy office was nothing like the primness she was used to at Smith and Brown, and Mr Blackie's dress and demeanour were nothing like that of her old and gentlemanly Mr Simmonite at Smith and Brown who wore a three-piece suit all year, whatever the weather, and was never known to remove his coat.

At first she found Mr Blackie to be gruff, almost rude, as he off-handedly described the duties of the job. But she concentrated as best she could knowing that if her application were successful the mysteries of the printing industry would no doubt reveal themselves in time and she would become part of William's trade. Even now, she thought, probably at this very minute, William is working as a respected and well-paid tradesman at Crosthwaite & Scott in New Plymouth.

'Girl Friday,' Mr Blackie was saying. 'Not my choice. Strange I know. But Tricky insisted.' Barbara had no idea who Tricky was. 'Said it's a modern term for the job. Have a look at this.'

He handed Barbara a quarto piece of yellow bond upon which was typed a list of the duties of a Girl Friday at Hervey-Harrison.

'Mrs Mac, she had to leave,' said Mr Blackie. 'Husband got ill. Cancer of the something. Anyway, afore she left she typed out what she did there—' he pointed to the sheet of paper Barbara was holding, ready to read '—and said if you want to know anything you can ring her up on her number at the bottom.'

Still confused — had Mr Blackie just handed her the job as he handed her the paper? — she quickly scanned the simple list before taking time to read it carefully, one bulleted item at a time.

Finished, she looked up to Mr Blackie who appeared to be waiting almost anxiously for her response. She assumed he was the Mr B referred to in Mrs Mac's list although she had no idea who Mrs H and Derek were; she assumed, though, that Kay was the receptionist and that "the boys" was Mrs Mac's name for the printers.

Whoever they all were she was confident that, based on the duties described in the list, being a Girl Friday for Hervey-Harrison would not be onerous. On the contrary, she thought she would manage it easily. She returned the list to Mr Blackie, smiled and nodded to show her understanding.

'Good,' he said emphatically. 'Now you don't have to worry about making tea for smoko, or getting the boys' lunches or anything like that,' he said as if he thought they were chores that *might* have been on the list. 'Young Colin takes care of all that stuff. Youngest apprentice etcetera. Know what I mean?'

Barbara nodded. She didn't know what he meant but it didn't seem to matter.

'And who would be my superior, Mr Blackie?' she asked.

'Superior what?'

'My manager, Mr Blackie? My boss? Who would be my boss?'

'Oh, that? Well, young lady,' replied Mr Blackie with a warm smile. At last, thought Barbara. 'I suppose that'd be yours truly.'

'I see,' said Barbara.

'And Mrs Harrison sometimes I suppose,' added the interviewer.

Obviously, thought Barbara, the Mrs H of the list. Nevertheless she asked: 'Mrs Harrison?'

'One of the owners,' said Mr Blackie. 'Important. Comes in sometimes. Once a week usually. On the list. Signs cheques and so on. Nothing to worry about.'

'I see,' said Barbara.

'There's Kay, the receptionist lass, you met her, answers the phone,' continued the interviewer, 'and Derek, Derek Skinner that is. Estimator. Bean-counter pen-pusher type. Quiet chap. But clever as billy-o. Keeps to himself. Wouldn't say boo to a goose. I'll introduce you in a minute.

'But the fact of the matter is,' he continued, leaning back in his chair and fiddling with a pencil, 'Mrs Mac — Mrs McAuley that was — well, she didn't need a boss. She did everything just fine. On her own. So if you're anything like her, Barbara — I *can* call you Barbara I suppose — you'll just get on and do things without a fuss. That's what I'd like. And if you don't, well, it'll be the Great Order of the Boot if you know what I mean.'

That last statement — the longest Barbara had heard from the man that morning — was said with another kindly smile which Barbara took to mean she was being given the job and that Mr Blackie was confident she would be at least as good a young Girl

Friday as Mrs Mac had been an old and old-fashioned do-everything office secretary.

Having settled on a wage better than Barbara expected, a little more than she had received at Smith and Brown, and having agreed that she would start the following Monday, Mr Blackie stood up and said he should show her around the factory.

'Different departments and people,' he said. 'Your office and doings. Telephone, typewriter, files etcetera. Ladies' toilet, lunchroom, all that sort of thing.'

Chapter 13

Barbara's office was a spacious room, beyond the main entry and reception, where Mr Blackie introduced her properly to the young receptionist as they passed through. She — Kay Coulson was her name — seemed both friendly and efficient although Barbara knew that her bouffant hair-style, pink lipstick, and her fashionably flouncy frock, supported by an unknown number of stiff petticoats, would not have been tolerated at Smith and Brown. Nevertheless, it seemed to Barbara that Kay Coulson was probably just "right" for receiving customers and visitors to the firm, in person and on the phone, surprising herself that she even had an opinion on such a matter.

At the far end of the open office space, at a desk in front of a wall of filing cabinets, was Derek Skinner, the estimator. Barbara didn't know but could guess the role of an estimator in a printing business.

Derek stood up when Mr Blackie introduced her. He looked awkward, embarrassed, and literally didn't know what to say. Barbara felt a little sorry for him. He was tall and thin and boyish looking; his pallid face was acne-scarred, and still as spotty as an adolescent's although Barbara guessed he was in his forties. His hair was shiny with too much brilliantine, and he wore old-fashioned horn-rimmed spectacles. He was wearing a woollen tartan tie and a maroon hand-knitted cardigan. Barbara thought he was a remarkably plain man, altogether devoid of personality. Little did she know then that the quiet unassuming Derek Skinner had an untapped talent for numbers, never tested by his job, which he would later apply willingly, when asked, to support Barbara's financial initiatives.

As Mr Blackie opened the office door to the factory he let in a dense concentration of the odours which the world finds offensively strong, printers hardly notice, and Barbara was beginning to like with a fondness she associated with William. Similarly, she was struck by a barrage of industrial sounds in which were blended pitches low and high and everything in between which the human hearing organs are capable of discerning and which Barbara relished only because she knew they were the same cacophonic combination that would be familiar to William.

'You'll get used to it,' shouted Mr Blackie although Barbara thought she was used to it already.

A pretty and smiling twenty-four year old woman, dressed and gloved and made-up for an important interview, naturally attracted a lot of attention — not all of it innocent — from the printers and labourers, young and old, bored by the firm's familiar females including their old Mrs Mac, Kay the receptionist — who gave as good as she got in the earthy-comments department — the middle-aged and irritable Mrs Gardner, and the so-called "ladies" of the bindery department.

As she hurried along after Mr Blackie, Barbara was acutely aware of the men's stares and what was implied by them.

So was Mr Blackie.

'Take no notice of them, love,' he said. 'They're harmless.'

Evidently, despite the attention Barbara's factory tour attracted from the busy overalled men, there were only six people Barbara needed to meet and know before she started work.

'Getting to know all the boys will come in due course,' said Mr Blackie referring, Barbara knew, to the factory staff. 'There's also Mrs Harrison,' he added. 'She's not here right now but you'll meet her next week. Don't worry about that.'

The letterpress department — Barbara remembered that William was a letterpress printer — was that part of the factory immediately outside the main office extending back to the far end of the building. Another glassed-in office, immediately adjacent to

Mr Blackie's but smaller, was that of the letterpress foreman, Ernie Richards. But he wasn't in his office. He was busy in the factory, preoccupied, when Mr Blackie approached with Barbara. He looked reluctant to stop what he was doing — standing beside a machine discussing something with one of his printers — but he stepped forward to listen to Mr Blackie's introduction, acknowledge Barbara, and wish her well.

From there she followed Mr Blackie past two ominous-looking guillotines — one large and one *very* large — into the offset department which even Barbara could see contained machines of a different size and type acting in a different manner from their letterpress brothers while making distinctly different noises.

Unlike Ernie Richards, Graham Cutler, the offset foreman, was young and handsome. And, again unlike inky-overalled Ernie, he was smartly dressed in taupe slacks, brown suede loafers, a cream shirt and pale blue tie. And he had a full head of thick brown hair. He wasn't on the factory floor, with his men and machines, but working at his desk in his own elevated and glassed-in office.

Barbara realized, as soon as he spoke, that he was English; she could also discern — she didn't know how — that he was vain and ambitious. She wasn't sure whether she should like him, or trust him, but he was friendly enough.

'You can call me Graham,' he said with a wink, 'if I can call you Barbara.'

Barbara couldn't help smiling at that, knowing that even fake charm is still charming.

The last stop on the tour was to the bindery department, which was separated from the printing departments by a sound-proof wall, at the other end of the factory.

The bindery manager — not a foreman, forewoman or forelady — was Mrs Gardner whom Barbara guessed to be about the age of her mother and aunt. Unlike her all-female staff, Mrs Gardner was dressed as if for a special outing to town, sans gloves, hat and handbag. She stood up, on high heels, when Mr Blackie and Barbara came to her desk and seemed to demand their full attention; Barbara sensed at once that Mr Blackie was intimidated by her. She shook Barbara's hand vigorously, Barbara's first and only handshake of the day, and said that she looked forward to them working together.

Barbara liked her at once.

Before they left the bindery department Mr Blackie opened the lunchroom door to give Barbara a quick look. She noticed only that it was furnished with cheap-looking red Formica tables and unmatched chairs — she couldn't help comparing it to the elegance of Smith and Brown's staff cafeteria — and that it had a few windows which looked out onto busy Burleigh Street.

Doors to the men's and women's toilets were beside the lunchroom, a fact that Mr Blackie pointed out with not a little embarrassment.

On the way back through the factory — Mr Blackie wanted to show Barbara the cart dock where paper deliveries were received and orders despatched — Barbara attracted more stares and whispered comments from Mr Blackie's "boys".

'Ignore them,' said Mr Blackie again. 'They'll get used to you.'

He then explained that Tricky Tremaine was out, wouldn't be back for a while, and so Barbara would have to wait until Monday to meet him.

'He's a bit of dag, is Tricky,' said Mr Blackie. 'You'll soon see. But he's a good bloke, a good salesman, and the customers like him so that's the main thing.'

Apart from his nickname — which made him sound somewhat of a dubious character anyway — Barbara had no mental picture of Tricky Tremain the salesman. The only salesmen she'd ever known were Smith and Brown's own showroom salesmen who were invariably tall, somewhat elderly, expensively dressed and shod, painfully supercilious and insincere, and the various travellers representing the country's finest brands of imported carpets, home furnishings and lighting, who had always treated her with the greatest respect.

'Now, the boys work factory hours, eight till half-past four, except Tuesdays and Thursdays when there's sometimes overtime,' continued Mr Blackie. 'Saturdays, too, sometimes. But you can start at half past eight and stay till five like me and Kay, Derek and Tricky. Office hours, see. Suits the customers that way.'

'I see,' said Barbara. 'Monday at half-past eight then.'

By then they were at the cart dock at the far end of the factory.

'Another way out,' he explained. 'Yes, love. See you Monday. And by the way,' he added, 'you'll be fine. I can tell. You'll fit in just fine.'

'Thank you, Mr Blackie. Thank you very much. See you Monday then.'

Mr Blackie nodded and waited to see her safely down the cart dock steps. Barbara was aware of his watching as she awkwardly, in high heels, stepped tentatively down the steep steps to street level making a mental note to always in future use the main door. She didn't turn around but nevertheless correctly guessed that her new boss was still watching as she turned down Burleigh Street, not able to imagine what a hugely important role, for good and not, *Hervey-Harrison Commercial Printers Ltd, Letterpress & Offset Printers, Burleigh Street, No Job Too Big or Small*, was to play in her future — and, incidentally, William's — and thus the countless times she was destined to make the short return journey between there and Brockley Cottage.

Chapter 14

It was William's older cousin Cedric who introduced him to New Plymouth's social life. And it was the result of Cedric's efforts that William came to meet the beautiful and irrepressible girl who was destined to become his wife. It was, however, one introduction which Cedric later regretted while denying all responsibility for its consequences.

It started innocently enough with an invitation to a party.

William had long ago joined Cedric at the Pukekura Park tennis club, so when he returned to New Plymouth at the end of December, after an indolent Christmas in Mount Eden, he was looking forward to a game. But as so many club members were away on holiday, and as most businesses were closed until the middle of January, things were especially quiet on the morning of the last day of nineteen sixty, a Saturday, when he met Cedric for a friendly game.

It was later, as they sat in the shade, on an old bench outside the clubrooms, recovering, that Cedric asked William what he was doing that night, New Year's Eve.

'No plans, really,' said William as he vigorously wiped his forehead and face with a towel.

'Well have I got news for you, young man,' said Cedric. 'A New Year's Eve shindig to end them all. And you're coming.'

The New Year's Eve party was indeed a big "shindig". It was held at a farm on the outskirts of Ōakura. The farmer-cum-host was a friend of Cedric, and the numerous partygoers were a mix of New Plymouth townies, neighbouring farmers, workers from the local dairy factories, and all their respective girlfriends, fiancés and spouses. The farmer's house — grand and sprawling as it was — could not accommodate all the guests and so the party had spilled out onto the deck, into the warm night, and from there down three wide steps onto the farmer's lawn which was fenced off from the three-hundred or so cows, the source of the farmer's considerable wealth.

It was a noisy affair which didn't matter as all the farmer's neighbours were in attendance, contributing their own voices to the commotion, and whose own homes were set well beyond the hearing range of any humans — mostly children — who slept their way into the new year.

It was there, at that party, on the expansive lawn of a Taranaki farm, that calm summer night, as nineteen sixty became nineteen sixty-one, that William was taught to dance the twist to the eponymous song, sung by one Chubby Checker, so often that he learned and never forgot the dance, the tune or the lyrics.

His dance teacher, who seemed to know everybody there while William knew no one but Cedric and his wife, seemed to purposely choose William for her party companion. William didn't know why but nor did he mind; although she was older than he, she was good company. He soon learned, however, from the rings on her finger before she confessed, that she was married — to a local dairy farmer — and was the mother of two young children. Evidently, according to her, her husband was 'so bloody boring, no sense of fun' who, rather than spending the night with his wife, singing and dancing, preferred to join his farmer friends in the kitchen where they remained all night drinking themselves drunk.

The party ended abruptly when the grey eastern horizon turned brilliant orange and so sent the reluctant unsober farmers and their wives, laughing and stumbling to their cars and home.

Even at dawn on New Year's Day, after a night of uninhibited drinking, partying, laughing and joking, singing and dancing, and so unburdening themselves of another year of hard physical work and mental stress — which is the lot of anyone whose living depends on the land and the weather — the farmers were compelled to report to their moaning milk-laden ladies who were already waiting impatiently for the relief only their owners' rhythmic sucking and clicking milking machines could provide. And so, even that morning, the weary farmers, young and old, did their duty while nursing aching heads and churning stomachs.

Meanwhile their wives — including William's new farmer's-wife friend Lois — were equally driven to their kitchens to prepare the mighty cooked hot breakfast demanded by the farmer and his hands even after a raucous New Year's Eve party. The man's breakfast was followed by a sweaty dreamless sleep broken only by the angry call of the afternoon's milking alarm clock.

And so began another year for the dairy farmers of Taranaki and New Zealand.

Once the party was over William's high spirits left him. He felt an overwhelming weariness. Cedric and Pat, too, felt the same and so little was said on the tedious drive home under an increasingly red-streaked dawn sky.

William did manage to ask about Lois. He didn't know her other name but it didn't matter; Cedric and Pat knew exactly whom he was asking about.

'That's Lois McCoombs,' said Pat. 'Lois Galvin that was.'

'Wouldn't get carried away, mate,' said Cedric. 'She's as married as hell. Got two kids.'

'She likes a bit of fun though,' said Pat.

'Mick, that's her old man,' said Cedric. 'He's a bit dour, real serious bloke.'

'He doesn't mind if she has a bit of fun, though,' said Pat. 'She's a real dag.'

'He's just the opposite,' said Cedric. 'Just lives and breathes farming.'

'It's just fun for her,' said Pat. 'Parties and that. She's devoted to him really.'

'And vice-versa,' said Cedric.

'I was only asking,' said William. 'Anyway, she's too old for me.'

'Do you *mind*,' said Pat with mock indignation. 'She's only thirty-eight or something. My age. Went to school together.'

'As I said,' said William, 'too old.'

They all had a laugh at that but no more was said that morning about Lois McCoombs or anyone or anything.

William's work friends, as well as those he had made at the tennis club and elsewhere, trickled back into town as the new year advanced until the social life of his fourth Taranaki summer was back to normal, the few days spent in Auckland almost forgotten. He had three weeks of holiday to enjoy which he did, doing something different and active with someone different every day.

He was still living in Brooklands with his Uncle Charles and Aunt Ruby who were, at that time, planning to sell their Devon Street stationery shop before retiring to Hamilton. They still treated William more like a son than a visiting nephew, and said he'd be welcome to move with them when they left town. But William felt settled in New Plymouth, happy in his job. He knew, therefore, that he would soon have to find a place of his own.

He didn't know what to do about that. Eventually he decided that, as the problem was spoiling his wonderful bachelor summer of nineteen sixty-one, he would ignore it until he no longer could.

At morning tea one hot morning in February, when William and a few colleagues were sitting outside in the shade, bare-chested, their overalls rolled down to the waist, smoking, drinking their tea, and chatting idly, hardly noticing the omnipresent Mount Egmont which dominated the city, Ngaire, the, firm's receptionist, came out into the sun, shading her eyes, to tell William that a lady was wating to see him in reception.

William's colleagues expressed their surprise, curiosity, even a sort of envy, with derisory but good-natured hoots, howls and whistles. Young Ngaire turned away then but not before pulling a face that graphically showed her disgust at the crude and mindless behaviour of young men when together in a group.

That same male ribbing caused William to blush slightly as he stood up and awkwardly pushed his arms into the sleeves of his inky overall, pulling it up properly in the process and quickly closing the domes before following Ngaire back to the reception lobby where he rarely ventured, especially in his overall.

'Who is it, Ngaire?' he asked as they walked together to the office.

'No idea,' said Ngaire curtly. Ngaire usually liked William but was still offended by the behaviour of the printers which, if she had only known it, was both typical of such a cohort, and utterly harmless. 'A woman that's all,' she said. 'Didn't say her name.'

Within a few weeks of that fateful day William found he was somehow going steady — that was the fashionable American term — with Jayne Galvin, the young sister of the gregarious and fun-loving Lois McCoombs, the Ōakura farmer's wife who had been his constant companion at the New Year's Eve party.

It was she, Lois, who was waiting for him in Ngaire's reception lobby that morning in early February, looking decidedly more frowsy and farmer's-wifely than he remembered. She said that rather than ring him up at "old Charlie Brockley's place", as she called it, she chose to be in town and visit him at work at morning tea time when she knew he'd be available.

'The thing is, Billy,' she said without ceremony, 'are you going to the Young Farmers' Saint Patrick's day tea dance?'

'Don't know anything about it,' said William truthfully.

'Oh, good,' said Lois. 'Well, the thing of it is, Jayne, that's my kid sister, not *that* young really, twenty, nearly twenty-one, bit of an accident mum-and-dad-wise if you get my drift. Well, thing of it is, she's dying to go but she hasn't got anyone to go with. No boyfriend and that.'

With no experience of clever women, unaware of their wiles and manipulative abilities when it came to innocent and vulnerable men like him, William had no idea why he was standing there in his overalls, awkwardly and out of place in the posh reception lobby of his employer, nor what the excited and breathless Lois

McCoombs, whom he had met only once, when they were both more than slightly inebriated, was actually talking about.

'I'm not sure what...' he said hesitatingly before being interrupted.

'The thing of it is, Billy,' Lois rushed on, 'would you like to meet her, Jayne that is, have a coffee or something? She lives in town with Mum and Dad. Up the top of Courtenay Street. And if you like her, if you get on, if she likes you too, I mean she's really pretty, and clever too, then...'

'You want me to take your sister to the Young Farmers' tea dance on Saint Patrick's day,' said William drily. 'Is that it?'

'That's it, Billy boy. Spot bloody on.'

William was intrigued but suspicious.

'If she's so pretty,' he asked with a questioning look, 'why hasn't she got a boyfriend?'

'Good question, Billy, but a longish story,' said Lois mysteriously. 'You don't want to know. Plus, she's a bit shy. The thing of it is, though, will you do it? I've told her all about you. Nice bloke and that. Tall, dark and handsome, etcetera. Just a couple of years older. So she's pretty keen.'

Chapter 15

A couple of days later, at a meeting, arranged by Lois McCoombs, in a Devon Street coffee bar near Morley Street, William sat down for an after-work meeting with Jayne Galvin. She was indeed pretty. William thought she was *very* pretty, beautiful even, just as Lois had said. But she definitely wasn't shy. On the contrary, she was even more excitably enthusiastic about everything than her extroverted sister. Whether she was as clever as Lois had said William couldn't tell from such a brief encounter.

'It's awfully embarrassing, Billy,' said Jayne with *faux* coyness. 'Lois made me do it, see. Match-making I suppose. A big sister type thing.'

'It's all right,' said William flatly. 'I don't mind.'

He couldn't help thinking of Barbara; how much more restrained and refined she would be if in the unlikely event she were in Jayne's place.

'And you don't mind about the dance?'

'No, I don't mind,' said William trying to sound interested. 'It'll be fun I suppose.'

'It *will* be fun,' said Jayne. 'It really *will*.'

They talked about their work. Jayne seemed interested in William's job.

'It's a printing place over in Morley Street,' he said. 'We print all sorts of things for customers all over Taranaki. Big jobs, too, sometimes.'

'Oh, I see,' said Jayne, apparently fascinated. 'But you're not a boss or anything?' she asked probingly.

'Me? God no,' said William. 'Just a worker.'

Jayne seemed disappointed. 'Bit like me I suppose,' she said.

'What do you mean?' asked William.

'Well, I work in a chemist shop don't I,' said Jayne. 'But I'm not a chemist. That's Mr Currie. Currie the Chemist. Just up the road.'

'By Currie Street,' said William. He knew the shop's owner, Noel Currie, from the tennis club.

'Yeah, but that's just a coincidence,' said Jayne. 'Anyway,' she continued, 'I like selling beauty products. I'm good at it too, you know. I've even done courses. I like Estée Lauder best. No, hang on. Max Factor. Yes, Max Factor's the best.'

The talk was small for a while until Jayne said she better go.

'Still live at home with Mum and Dad,' she said. 'Mum wants me home for tea, see.'

'So where's that?' asked William. 'The address I mean. I'll have to pick you up for the dance.'

'Oh yes,' said Jayne 'Silly me, eh.'

They exchanged addresses and phone numbers.

'It's at the old Hempton Hall in Ōkato,' said Jayne as she stood up. 'The dance. Do you know it?'

'I know it,' said William. 'Half hour drive, that's all.'

'Starts at six,' said Jayne 'Early for the farmers, see.'

'That's all right,' said William. 'I finish at half-past-four so I'll pick you up about half-past-five.'

'With your lovely big Zephyr,' said Jayne. 'I've seen you in it. Driving around town looking so cool and groovy.'

William had a sudden thought.

'Friday night,' he said. 'Aren't the shops open late Friday nights? Don't you have to work?'

'I'm going to wag it that day,' said Jayne with a grin. 'The whole day. Gonna be sick as anything.'

William was surprised; a little offended even.

They were on the street.

'Don't you dare tell old man Currie, though,' said Jayne as she grinningly wagged her forefinger in William's face.

William smiled and shook his head. He could help being amused by her jollity.

'See you on the seventeenth,' he said.

'It's a long time,' said Jayne 'More than two whole weeks. Can't we catch up before then?'

'Can't really,' said William without knowing why.

'Oh, well,' said Jayne with a shrug. 'See you then, eh. It'll be good.'

William found the Young Farmer's Saint Patrick's Day dance, in the old Ōkato hall, was good but might have been better if everyone had danced the same dance. Instead of the conventional dance, which he was used to, where the band leader announced each dance — *Ladies and Gentlemen, take your partners for a foxtrot / quickstep / waltz* — and all the paired dancers glided together, counter-clockwise around the hall, with more or less grace, in the time-honoured fashion, he found that, whatever the tune, tempo and rhythm of the music, only half the couples complied. The other half — mostly the younger ones including an enthusiastic Jayne, and William too — simply stayed where they stood to dance the new twist. Meanwhile, those older couples, earnestly executing their accustomed ballroom steps, had to manoeuvrer their way around the young twisters. William sensed the older — some very old — dancers' annoyance and felt sorry for them. But was glad he knew how to twist thanks to Jayne's sister Lois. She was also there, dancing mostly with everyone but her husband.

William enjoyed himself that night. He enjoyed meting Jayne's parents who seemed somewhat elderly to him, about the same age as his Uncle Charles. He enjoyed seeing Jayne looking so beautiful in her lovely white gown, trimmed with green, with a matching green Jackie band holding back her shoulder-length blonde hair. He enjoyed the way she was impressed by his car and how much she enjoyed the early evening drive south to Ōkato. And he especially enjoyed seeing how everyone, male and female, seemed to admire his beautiful and vivacious consort.

He realized only then — when he saw that Jayne was known by almost everyone there — that it wasn't he who was helping the reportedly shy and date-less Jayne by escorting her to the dance but that someone, probably Cedric, who was always questioning him about his lack of a girlfriend, had conspired with Lois to get Jayne to bring *him* to the dance and so meet more young people and improve his social life.

Knowing, then, that he had been cleverly manipulated, William decided he didn't mind. Indeed, he was glad. Jayne may have been a conspirator at first but she seemed to be enjoying his company. And he was pleased that, despite her popularity, she stayed at his side all night, proudly introducing him to her many friends while confidently making polite conversation with his few. He was flattered that she seemed to have curbed her natural high spirits to conduct herself with elegance and poise — for his sake, he assumed — in contrast to the loud and brash behaviour of her elder sister whose all-night skylarking could be heard all around the old hall.

Despite his doubts about his entertainment value as a dance companion and partner, William was glad to discover that Jayne must have enjoyed his company as much as he enjoyed hers when she suggested, on the drive home, that they should meet again. A week later, on a Saturday night, they went to the pictures, at the big Regent in Devon Street, just down the road from Jayne's workplace, where it was she who took and affectionately squeezed William's hand.

During and after that date, when, unlike the Young Farmers' dance, they were alone together, William couldn't help comparing Jayne to Barbara who was never far from his thoughts. He thought Jayne acted a bit young for her age. She was, of course, younger than Barbara and him by five years. Perhaps, he thought, she was a spoiled younger child, being an accidental late-comer to her parents. On the other hand he found her almost-teenage outlook on life to be new and refreshing, exposing him to people, places, thoughts and ideas which he might never have encountered without her. And he was flattered to find that she happily agreed with — and openly admired — *his* more mature views on the political and social affairs of New Plymouth, Taranaki, New Zealand and the world.

The opinions he expressed so willingly to his admiring listener were not entirely his but absorbed by listening to his older work colleagues. However, he was happy to let Jayne think he was more clever and mature than perhaps he really was.

On the Tuesday of the week before Easter, William received an evening phone call from Jayne.

'Lois and Mick want us to come to dinner on Saturday night,' she said.

'That's Easter Saturday,' said William.

'I know,' said Jayne 'Long weekend holiday. Isn't that neat.' William thought she sounded unreasonably excited by the thought. 'Anyway,' she continued, 'they said they want to get to know you better. I said that would be all right. Do you mind, Billy?'

William wasn't sure why Jayne's older sister and brother-in-law wanted to get to know him at all, but couldn't immediately think of an objection.

'No,' he said. 'Don't mind. Where do they live?'

'Got a big farm half way down Lower Pitone Road,' said Jayne 'Do you know where that is?'

'I know,' said William.

'Will you pick me up, Billy? About half-past five. Early I know but Mick doesn't do late nights.'

'Okay,' said William flatly. 'See you then.'

'Was that that Jayne Galvin again?' asked his aunt when he was off the phone.

William nodded.

'Works at Curries?'

'That's her,' said William. He knew Currie's and the Brockley's stationery shop were neighbours.

'She your girlfriend now?'

William thought his normally kind and tolerant aunt sounded mildly judgemental. He shrugged. *Was* Jayne his girlfriend? Is that what Aunt Ruby thought?

'I suppose so,' he said as casually as he could and was then puzzled by his aunt's slight frown, pinched lips and faint but unmissable head-shake. Obviously she didn't approve of Jayne Galvin but he didn't know why and didn't ask.

The early dinner at the McCoombs' farm was more enjoyable than William had expected. Lois's excitable behaviour, always so loud and commanding, seemed perfectly normal and natural in her own home. And Mick, her evidently quiet husband, seemed to be devoted to her; they seem to be devoted to each other. William thought them the perfect loving couple. Evidently they had children, a boy and girl — William saw photographs about the house — but they were not at dinner and were not mentioned.

Farmer Mick McCoombs, whom William had expected to be especially serious about everything, conversant in nothing but dairy farming — about which William knew nothing — was the perfect host, interesting, and interested in William's life, his family, his work in New Plymouth, and his opinions. William thoroughly enjoyed his company and conversation.

By the time dinner was over, and the guests were preparing to go, William felt that a strange bond had been formed between him and the McCoombs couple; he liked and admired them both and somehow knew that they liked and admired him in return.

'Did you have a nice time tonight, Billy?' asked Jayne as they joined the highway home.

'Yeah,' said William. 'It was good. I enjoyed it.'

Later, in the back seat of the car, parked in a remote country lane on the coast, William discovered that the young, excitable, enthusiastic and fun-loving Jayne Galvin was equally excitable, enthusiastic and unrestrained in matters of physical love. And considerably more experienced than he.

'Just as well I work at a chemist's,' she said with a laugh as she unashamedly drew a sealed *Durex* from her evening bag.

And then, having completely abandoned herself to physical pleasure, she routinely patted her hair into shape, rearranged her underwear and dress, and sighed.

'Oh, Billy,' she said, rolling her eyes, 'that was absolutely groovy.'

'You can say that again,' said a hot, puffing and astonished William as he too clumsily set about tucking in his shirt and otherwise returning things below the waist to normal.

'Now,' said Jayne, 'you better get me home before Mum and Dad start worrying.'

Meanwhile, in faraway Mount Eden, a happy and newly-healthy Barbara Conwyne, having been five weeks into her Girl Friday job at Hervey-Harrison, spent that Easter Saturday night with her mother and aunt, innocently enjoying the novelty of television with their new television set — bought from the Farmers with a staff discount — before settling down to sleep, safe and secure in her Brockley Cottage bedroom.

Chapter 16

Barbara settled easily and quickly into her new job; any misgivings she might have had evaporated after her first day when she found that the duties listed so carefully by the retired Mrs McAuley — whom she never met and never had reason to contact — were not hard. Mr Blackie mostly left her to her own devices, and the office atmosphere was refreshingly relaxed compared with what she had known at Smith and Brown. She was able to dress more informally than was permitted at Smith and Brown which, given the grimy, dusty, fumy and inky atmosphere of a printing factory, was sensible as well as being comfortable.

Mr Blackie, whom she found slightly intimidating at her interview, proved to be a kind and considerate manager who treated her more like a daughter than an employee; he rarely asked about her work or interfered in any way. Nor did he seem interested in her home life or personal circumstances, which suited her.

Mrs Harrison, whom she met on her first Thursday morning, when the old lady came in for a meeting with Mr Blackie, and to sign the wages cheque, explained a few things to Barbara during a "wee chat" they had after her meeting. She explained that she had inherited the firm from her late husband, that she knew nothing about printing but a lot about business and people, and that she trusted Mr Blackie to run a "tight ship".

'I keep my nose out of the details, dear,' she said.

Barbara learned later that Mr Blackie was married to Mrs Harrison's only child, a daughter called Heather, and that he and

Heather had only one child, a Down Syndrome daughter called Mary-Jane whom Mrs Blackie treasured and protected.

Mrs Harrison always addressed her son-in-law as Mr Blackie while he always addressed her as Mrs Harrison. Barbara thought it quaint but inevitable; he could hardly call her Mum or Mother in the office or at a meeting.

Tricky Tremaine was out of the office most of the day and yet Barbara enjoyed his company more than anyone's. She soon learned that despite his nickname he wasn't at all tricky. Tricky was one of those nicknames of irony like calling a short man Lofty, a fat man Slim, or a red-haired man Blue. In fact Tricky Tremaine was remarkably honest; sometimes, it was said, too honest. He was also, as Barbara discovered, a kind, considerate, decent and generous young man, qualities which meant he was popular with his colleagues as well as, importantly, with his customers who trusted him and his word.

'Don't know what we'd do without this young fella,' said Mr Blackie, tapping Tricky lightly on the shoulder as he introduced him to Barbara on her first day. 'Best print salesman in town bar none.'

She learned that Tricky's real name was Trevor and guessed he was about her age; in fact he was twenty-six, a year older than she. He was not especially tall, but definitely handsome, athletic and well-built, with black eyes, a dark complexion and black wavy hair. And unlike all the other men, in the office and factory — including Mr Blackie and Derek — he always wore a smart suit with a white shirt and tie, and highly-polished shoes.

At first meeting Barbara thought he favoured Tony Curtis, the movie star she had seen in *Spartacus*. Kirk Douglas was the star of that movie but she and the twins agreed that Tony Curtis was much better looking.

Tricky's resemblance to the movie star faded as Barbara got to know him better until she didn't notice it at all. She was surprised though to learn that he was single, like her, and, also like her, that he lived at home, in Waterview, with his widowed mother.

Of the other people she had to deal with daily, Barbara found that her first impressions were consistently confirmed.

Unfortunately, Kay Coulson, the young receptionist, quickly came to regard Barbara as an older sister. She often shared intimate details of her relations with her young fiancé Ricky, sometimes seeking advice about her forthcoming wedding night and married life which Barbara felt utterly ill-equipped to provide.

It took her longer to know the factory staff. Seeing working-class men of all ages, working together for eight hours or more a day, five days or more a week, sharing their breaks in the lunchroom where they talked loudly and constantly — about what, she didn't know — was a new experience. But she did begin to understand the camaraderie which working men share. She assumed it was what William had enjoyed at the Farmers, when he was there, and which she hoped he was enjoying again in New Plymouth.

Close to Christmas the Hervey-Harrison social club arranged a Friday night dine-and-dance party at the Sorrento, in Cornwall Park, for staff, spouses and girlfriends, to which Tricky was her escort and principal dance partner. And then, on the afternoon of the next day, there was a Christmas party in the factory lunchroom for the children and grandchildren of the staff, where big "Dutchy" Bax played Santa Claus, handing out gifts, which Barbara had helped buy and wrap, from under the tree which Barbara had helped to decorate.

It was then, as the year ended so socially, that Barbara realized how happy, truly happy, she was at Hervey-Harrison.

'I had no idea work could be so much fun,' she said to her mother. 'I mean, compared to Smith and Browns.'

Mildred was happy for her, not only for the enjoyment she got from her work but also because whatever had caused her awful ill health — her breakdown — had not returned. Barbara was not only happy but obviously healthy, a state of well-being which she herself ascribed to the contentment she found at work.

And so, Barbara's year of nineteen sixty-one passed quickly. So quickly that she was surprised and disappointed when the factory finally closed, for the summer holidays, on the Friday before Christmas; it wasn't scheduled to reopen until Monday the sixteenth of January in the new year.

As usual, the waitressing twins were required to work during those three weeks, except for the statutory holidays when the Farmers and all shops were closed. Barbara enjoyed being alone at home all day. Once again she happily spent the long and balmy summer days working in the garden, and doing small maintenance chores around the house.

She thought of William often, but no longer pined for him nor wondered hourly, as she once had, what he was doing in New Plymouth, and with whom, and whether or not he had a girlfriend, and if he did who she was and what she might look like and be like. Rather, she was glad to have resigned herself to the fact that although she truly loved William, perhaps more than a cousin should, and always would, he would undoubtedly, naturally, meet someone, get married and have children and grandchildren.

Although she knew *she* would never marry she could only wish the very best for him.

Having worked all day, in the garden or around the house, Barbara joined the tired twins in front of the television, to end the day quietly, before going to bed early, healthily tired and satisfied.

Her routine was broken only once, early in the new year but before the factory reopened, when Tricky Tremaine asked her if she'd like to go on a picnic.

'Just you and me, Barbs,' he said on the phone. 'Nothing romantic or anything like that. Just a nice day out with a friend.'

And that's exactly what it was: a *very* nice day out with a friend. A friend who had prepared a lovely picnic.

'It's a lovely picnic, Trevor,' she said.

'Well, mum helped,' admitted Tricky.

Barbara and Tricky's was a true friendship, not just at work, with never the slightest hint of romance which pleased Barbara and evidently suited Tricky. Not that the subject of romance wasn't broached; it was explored that day, not in depth but enough to satisfy them both that it would not, could not, subvert their friendship.

'It's Mum, you see,' said Tricky. 'My dad died years ago, when I was a kid. Only ten. Fact is, I hardly remember him. But *she* can't forget him and there's only me and I remind her of him all the time. Awkward really. Now she's getting on, fifty-seven, and not very well so I just can't leave her, see. Not for another woman. No offence. But she'd never forgive me.'

Barbara thought it strange that Tricky's mother, at fifty-seven, was only seven years older than her own mother and aunt neither of whom showed any hint of advancing age or illness. Still, she sympathized with both mother and son as — she explained to Tricky — she was only nine when her father was killed. And although she hardly remembered him she remembered how sad her mother was for so long.

'And what about you?' asked Tricky.

'I *was* really properly in love once,' Barbara replied willingly. 'Still am I suppose.'

'So what happened?' asked Tricky.

'Oh, it's *impossible,*' she replied with a resigned sigh. She lay back then, her hands clasped behind her head, and looked vacantly, dreamily, up through the tangle of the trees into the deep blue of the clear sky, thinking of William. 'Absolutely impossible,' she added.

Tricky sensed her sadness. 'I understand,' he said. 'I really do.' Barbara sensed his own secret sadness then. 'But why?' he asked.

Barbara could tell he was genuinely interested. And sympathetic. But she didn't want sympathy.

'Oh, Trevor,' she said, suddenly checking her sentimentality by sitting up to straighten her dress and check her hair. She rested back on her elbows. 'It's really such a long story.'

Tricky shrugged to suggest that he wouldn't press her for an explanation. Nevertheless, Barbara felt she owed him something more. And so she added: 'I might tell you one day. When the time is right.'

The vague explanations they gave each other that lovely summer Wednesday, so long ago, about their personal lives, and the reason for their respective singleness, were never referred to again except once, but much later, when Barbara was forced to tearfully confess her love for William.

And while short and markedly over-simplified, the reasons given for their lovelessness were sufficient to satisfy each receiver about the other's vulnerability and sincerity and so cement their mutual trust which, although they didn't know it then, was to last a lifetime.

Chapter 17

When Barbara returned to work in the middle of January the weather was still hot, the factory even hotter. She knew that was the reason the holiday spirit spilled over into the first few weeks of the new year when the boys — as she had learned to refer to the printers — looking especially fit and tanned, continued to share and compare stories of their holidays. Even Mr Blackie confided in her — and no one else — that he and Mrs Blackie spent the holidays at their Red Beach bach where their daughter Mary-Jane was happy and safe.

Barbara was less pleased with the confidence imparted by Kay Coulson who confessed that she and Ricky had been camping together at Waihi Beach, sleeping together in a little tent.

'And no one took a blind bit of notice,' she said. 'Oh, Barbs, it was *amazing.*'

Barbara was no longer shocked by anything Kay said or did but couldn't show approval or share her enthusiasm.

'It'll be amazing if you get pregnant,' she said. 'Then what?'

To which Kay merely waved her hand dismissively and said a long 'Ooooh, Barbs,' as if hardly believing anyone could be so old-fashioned and not thrilled by the news of her daring naughtiness.

Eventually holiday talk was forgotten and the factory returned to the routine which Barbara valued. She still, in a vague but nevertheless constant way, embraced the notion that by working at Hervey-Harrison, and mixing with the men of the printing trade, she had something in common — a shared experience — with William.

She still thought of him often, with a fondness which had never diminished, and although their correspondence had fallen away, as it had between William and his mother, they exchanged birthday cards on the due dates in which they each included a snippet of their own news, innocent and trivial.

Nevertheless, it came as a complete shock one Saturday morning, in the middle of February, when William's mother received not a letter from William but a fancy envelope from New Plymouth addressed in an unknown hand.

The three women of Brockley Cottage were sitting together in the kitchen, taking a break from their Saturday morning housekeeping with a cup of tea.

Millicent opened the envelope. Inside was an invitation to William's wedding, addressed to them all.

None had the slightest idea that William was engaged or even had a steady girlfriend. But there it was: a cream satin-finished card, delicately deckle-edged on one side, featuring, on the front, a blind-embossed rose, its stem embellished with a tiny and shiny silver bow.

It was an item of personal social stationery which impressed Barbara's professional printer's eye in a way that escaped the twins' notice; they were simply bemused by its mere existence and arrival.

Inside, printed in silver — with the personalized lines elegantly written out in cursive, using a matching silver ink — was the text of the invitation for the three taken-aback women to read, aloud and silently, again and again:

Mr and Mrs Henry J. Galvin
of Courtenay Street, New Plymouth
have much pleasure in inviting

Mesdames Mildred and Millicent

Conwyne

and

Miss Barbara Conwyne

& Partners

to the wedding of their darling younger daughter
Jayne Elizabeth
to
William Robert Conwyne
of New Plymouth, formerly of Auckland,
on Saturday 21st April, 1962, at 2 o'clock in the afternoon
at Saint Mary's Church, 37 Vivian Street, New Plymouth
followed by a breakfast to be held at
The Taranaki Club, 1 Queen Street, New Plymouth

R.S.V.P. by Friday 30 March, 1962.

A small matching card and envelope were also enclosed by which the invitees could and should respond.

'Partners!' Millicent almost shouted the word. 'Me?'

'That'll be the day,' said Mildred with a laugh.

'I'll take Trevor,' said Barbara quietly.

'That's only two months or something,' said Mildred.

'I know what that means,' said Millicent knowingly.

'Young people these days,' said Mildred, clicking her tongue with a smiling pretence of disapproval. 'I think that's Easter weekend,' she added.

'Silly boy,' said Millicent who couldn't repress a smile. 'Fancy that, though. Me, a grandmother.'

'A dreaded mother-in-law first,' said Mildred.

'Get away,' said Millicent. 'Anyway, we'll have to go all the way to New Plymouth.'

'Catch up with Charles and Ruby at last,' said Mildred. 'And all the family I suppose.'

'My God,' said Millicent. 'Mother of the groom. What on earth shall we wear?'

They remembered then that the Farmers ladies' department was planning a summer clearance sale in anticipation of its autumn collection.

'We'll look double posh,' said Millicent, meaning they would both buy and wear the same *ensembles*: frocks, hats, gloves, shoes and handbags.

And that set the two of them laughing.

Meanwhile Barbara took the invitation through to the parlour where she checked the date on the calendar before going out to the side veranda where she sat on the porch's old wickerwork swing chair. There, swinging gently, she was able to closely study the invitation's words.

Jayne Elizabeth they said. Jayne Elizabeth Galvin.

So, she thought, my darling William Robert Conwyne is marrying someone called Jayne Elizabeth Galvin. Jayne Galvin. I wonder what on earth she's like. Of all the women in the world, or in New Plymouth for that matter, why did William choose Jayne Elizabeth Galvin? Or, did she choose him? Is she pregnant? That's what Mummy and Auntie Millie think. So is she one of those wily women who allow themselves to get pregnant — who *want* to get pregnant — so the man of their choice will *have* to marry them? I've heard of that. Is that what happened to poor William? Trapped by this clever Jayne person.

As she swung idly in her chair, turning over the invitation in her hands to inspect it closely, Barbara was amused again to find that she could professionally appreciate its quality. She wondered if William had printed it. And how many had been printed. And who was the bindery lady who must have carefully glued on the silly little bow.

Was it, she wondered, to be a big wedding? The tasteful and obviously expensive invitation suggested it would be a big and perhaps lavish affair ending at the posh-sounding Taranaki Club.

Poor William, she thought. But I suppose it had to happen one day. He's too nice and clever and handsome to *not* get married.

Surprised she wasn't more upset by the news, Barbara bounced out of the swing and, invitation in hand, returned to the dining room where the twins were still discussing outfits appropriate to the mother and aunt of the groom, in accordance with the season, early autumn in New Plymouth, the afternoon timing of the ceremony followed by photographs and a wedding reception which would undoubtedly, obviously, extend into the evening hours.

'It *is* Easter,' said Barbara, tossing the invitation on the table between the seated women. 'I checked.'

'Now, dear,' said her mother, 'Millie and I agree. We must all look our very best down there. For William's sake of course, in front of his new wife and her family, but also because your Uncle Charles and Aunt Ruby will be there and we haven't seen them for donkey's years and they haven't seen you since you were a wee tot so you must promise to look your absolute beautiful best.'

'They're always so judgemental,' added Millicent.

'And snobby,' said Mildred. 'All the more reason...'

'Oh, Mummy,' interrupted Barbara. 'Of course I'll look my best.' And then she added, surprising even herself with her spontaneous outburst: 'But isn't it EXCITING!'

By the time of the wedding Barbara had been at Hervey-Harrison for more than a year. She had a little car by then: a 1958 Austin A35, bought with the help and advice of Tricky Tremaine. However, despite being a confident and experienced town driver, she lacked confidence on country roads — especially the hilly and winding road to New Plymouth to which William often referred — so was glad when Mr Blackie said it would be all right for Tricky to take them all to New Plymouth in his company car.

Chapter 18

Four years later, on a cold and rainy Saturday morning in the middle of August, nineteen sixty-six, William and his somewhat moody wife were on their way to Auckland, in their new Holden, to celebrate Barbara's thirtieth birthday in July, William's in September; a shared birthday dinner with the three Auckland women who hadn't seen them since their wedding and whom Jayne barely knew.

Despite Jayne's reluctance, William had planned and started the journey hopefully.

'We always had a shared birthday party when we were kids,' he explained to Jayne. 'And now, the big three-oh. Can hardly believe it.'

It wasn't true that he and Barbara had always shared a birthday party, but for William it was easier than trying to again explain, to his possessive and petulant wife, the close and loving relationship he had with his girl cousin in Auckland. In fact he was inordinately excited about the trip, more than he could let on to Jayne, not only because he was suddenly anxious to see Barbara again, and his mother to a lesser degree, but also because they would be staying upstairs, in his old bedroom, in dear old Brockley Cottage which, despite its dilapidation, contained many happy memories.

He doubted he'd be able to share his memories and sentiments with Jayne who never showed any interest in his family; for some reason she seemed to resent their very existence. It was a reaction he didn't understand especially as he had embraced *her* family and had eventually and happily been fully accepted by them.

Nevertheless, he had learned to keep comments about Barbara, his mother and aunt — but especially Barbara — and Brockley Cottage, to a minimum.

He also knew, or guessed, that his mother, aunt and cousin had not entirely approved of Jayne when they met her at the wedding. And although his mother and Barbara wrote occasionally — not often — they rarely asked about Jayne.

And so, on the long drive north, William secretly hoped that Jayne would be as friendly and outgoing — vivacious even — as he knew she could be and usually was, especially with strangers, and would come to at least like if not love his female family. He hoped that they, in turn, would see the Jayne who was so well-known and popular in New Plymouth, and at least accept her at last as his wife.

William had changed a lot in the years since the wedding, not all of it for the better.

Even before the wedding, having suffered the ire of Jayne's father, things were not easy when he had to let his mother know that her brother Charles and his wife had retired, as planned, sold their stationery shop, and shifted to Hamilton to be near their daughter Betty and their grandchildren. As a result, Millicent and Mildred, who had assumed their party of four would be welcome to stay the long weekend at their brother's house, had to find other — paid — accommodation

It wasn't William's fault that his uncle and aunt had moved house at such an inconvenient time. But Millicent made her annoyance clear, especially when she learned that William didn't want his Auckland visitors to stay in his new house.

William had bought a small and affordable new house, in a Marfell Block subdivision — a heavily publicised "Parade of Homes" — in anticipation of his pending homelessness. He was living in the house in the few weeks before the wedding but had great difficulty convincing his mother that it was unready to receive guests; it was somewhat out of town, barely furnished, and he was sleeping in a sleeping bag on a mattress on the floor.

Turning the empty house into a proper home will be Jayne's job once we're married.' he wrote. 'Until then it's not ready for occupation.'

At the wedding, and afterwards at the reception, William *thought* his mother and aunt, and Barbara too — Barbara most importantly — approved of Jayne but, being the busy groom, he wasn't sure. He did see, however, that they got on well with Jayne's parents, especially with Mr Galvin who thought Barbara was charming and the middle-aged identically-dressed identical twins were exceptionally attractive and endearingly eccentric.

'Never met the likes of them in my whole life,' he said to Mrs Galvin later. 'Like a pair of bloody gypsies. Earrings, gold rings, chains and gems and jewels dangling and jangling all over the place. And so much black hair all sparkly. Half expected them to tell my fortune.'

For their part the three Auckland women, and Tricky, enjoyed themselves at the seaside Taranaki Club that Easter Saturday of nineteen sixty-two; Millicent told William so later in a letter of thanks sent when she got home.

Nevertheless, William sensed — knew — that his mother had doubts about Jayne and the wisdom of the marriage. He knew the obviously rushed wedding would be the source of her doubts, doubts which he assumed she had shared with her sister and Barbara. But she never asked him the obvious question and so he never offered the obvious explanation.

He also knew, without doubt, that Barbara didn't approve of Jayne either. He didn't know why but she seemed suspicious somehow. He saw she was barely civil to her at the reception and later, which was not like the usually kind and friendly Barbara he thought he knew.

On the other hand he so wanted to dislike the man she had brought with him — her partner for the occasion (or *all* occasions?) — but couldn't. He found Tricky Tremaine most agreeable and thought that he and Barbara were ideally suited which caused him to be mildly and unreasonably jealous, then and for some time later.

Jayne's pregnancy *was* of course the reason for the rushed wedding. It was also the reason William wasn't properly accepted by her disapproving parents although her sister and farmer brother-in-law, Lois and Mick McCoombs, had always liked William and were as supportive as they could be. However, despite almost universal suspicions, only Jayne's family *knew* the truth. But to guess the truth and then cheerfully go along with the charade in spite of all evidence, even after the event, was normal social behaviour at that time.

Despite widespread suspicion about the sudden marriage, and qualms about the chances of its success, William ignored the mostly unspoken judgement knowing that the scandal was petty, not uncommon, and would soon be forgotten.

He had decided, in the little time he had before the wedding, that it was about time he was married anyway and that Jayne, so beautiful — stunningly so on her wedding day, even Barbara admitted that — would surely make a good wife and mother. He knew she wasn't clever, was even a little naïve and childish in many ways, but she was usually cheerful, optimistic and kind, and easy to get along with, which he thought was important. And she seemed to love him — she said she did, often — which she promised to prove, physically and frequently, once they were married. And so he resolved to be a good husband, and a loving father to their unplanned but rapidly developing child, and to thereby gain the respect of his in-laws.

A brief honeymoon in Rotorua was planned after which William and Jayne were to return to Marfell to make a home for themselves and their baby. William was looking forward to returning to work while Jayne intended to resign from Currie's when her condition became obvious.

That was the newlyweds' plan. However, all was not obstetrically well.

Chapter 19

Jayne spent her honeymoon in Rotorua hospital as the result of a painful and frightening miscarriage on the second night of their stay in their Fenton Street motel. William was utterly perplexed by the shocking suddenness of the event, by Jayne's distress, the bloody mess — an awful reminder of another bloody mess — and then by having no idea how to comfort the hospitalized wife who, when she cried out only for her mother, he realized he hardly knew. And so he deferred to her mother and sister who both dashed across country when William told them what had happened.

Once out of hospital and back in New Plymouth, Jayne stayed a few weeks with her parents in Courtenay Street. She eventually returned to William feeling depressed and angry, and highly critical of the myriad choices William had been forced to make concerning the comforts and conveniences of their new Marfell home.

Her mental and physical health returned soon enough — she was in fact a remarkably fit and healthy young woman — and so, suddenly optimistic, she set about making the home *she* wanted, furnishing and equipping it in a way that William — or any man — never could. She also returned happily to her job at Currie's beauty counter, resuming her life there as if nothing untoward had happened. That she had acquired a new name with a new address and phone number was almost incidental to her, her employer, colleagues and customers.

That her belly didn't swell, and that no infant was ever delivered, confounded everyone except her family and William.

And although most mature and experienced women, who could recognize even the earliest signs of pregnancy, guessed what *must* have happened, most others — including Mr Currie and her colleagues, and William's colleagues and his family — assumed they must have been mistaken and that, after all, amazingly, William and Jayne's marriage was founded on true love.

Of course it wasn't.

The brave young couple did at first enjoy being married. While Jayne set about creating the type of fairy-tale home she had romantically dreamed of since girlhood, not at all appreciating how easy it was for her, without children, compared with her neighbours, William found he enjoyed being a suburban husband. He not only relished the hard physical labour required to break in a bare section but also the help he got from the new friends he made in the street and the help he was able to give them in return. Together they planned gardens, built fences, laid concrete drives and paths, installed rotary clothes lines and planted hedges and trees, all of which remained to be used and enjoyed by later generations who would have no idea of the struggle young people faced in that subdivision in nineteen sixty-two.

Jayne, too, made many new friends in their new street, Solebay Place, the young wives of William's helpmate friends, all of whom had young children or children on the way or both. As a result they — William and Jayne together — suddenly had a lively social life with neighbours who, burdened by mortgages and children, depended on each other for moral support as well as home-based friendship.

Sensitive William, though, soon realized they were different from their neighbours in many ways. They had two incomes, they didn't struggle to pay their mortgage but could afford things which others considered unaffordable luxuries, including a new Holden station wagon. And without children they were free to go anywhere, at any time, night or day.

And he saw — thinking of Jayne — that children, especially babies but *all* children, were a constant worry, especially to their mothers whose faces revealed the fears they tried to hide and whose bodies seemed to sag in unfashionable clothes, making them appear older than their age which was only a few years more than Jayne's. Jayne, less sensitive than William, did however note the effect that bearing and rearing children had on the faces, bodies, attitudes, temperaments and marriages of her young motherly neighbours.

William was so busy with life — his marriage, the house and garden and his work — that the next couple of years passed quickly. But eventually his property required only regular maintenance which was a pleasure rather than a chore and reminded him of the long-ago pleasant days he spent in the Brockley Cottage garden.

He even installed a greenhouse at the back of his Solebay Place house, where he raised his own flowers and vegetables, and that reminded him again of his young life in Mount Eden and of the happy and carefree years he spent there with Barbara.

He thought of Barbara often and wished he could see her and be with her if only for a brief visit. But Auckland seemed so far away.

Meanwhile he continued to do well at work and at the end of nineteen sixty-five, on the eve of his Christmas holidays, aged just twenty-nine, he was given a generous raise and promoted to foreman of his department.

'Keep it up, lad,' said Mr Scott, the managing director, 'and you'll have Harry's job before long.'

Harry was Harry McCorquindale, the firm's production manager who was due to retire at the end of the following year.

As life became easier for William he began picking up the activities and friends he had abandoned, partly at Jayne's insistence, partly of necessity, when he got married.

Tennis was his first love but he also resumed sailing with yachting friends and tramping the high bush trails of Mount Egmont. He also rejoined the New Plymouth Golf Club where he spent a lot of time, made a lot of new friends, and enjoyed a busy social life.

Jayne, though, felt awkward in the company of *her* old friends. Like her young married neighbours in Solebay Place they seemed to be obsessed with matters that didn't concern her: their husbands' careers and income, sex, their children's health, their domestic worries, and the high cost of everything.

She was grateful to William for taking her to every dinner, dance, barbecue, prize-giving, house-warming and other occasion or event to which he was invited or of which he was a party. There, at William's side, she discovered a new set of people: William's old and many new friends who were older, more successful, wealthier, more interesting and more influential than the now-married and fretful friends of her single days.

The beautiful, charming, vivacious, popular — and, it must be said, sexy — young Jayne Galvin was now the beautiful, charming, vivacious, popular, and still undeniably sexy Jayne Conwyne whom older men found especially attractive. Their wives, however, eyed Noel Currie's well-known young assistant with a mixture of envy and suspicion appropriate to her rumoured reputation.

It was a happy and carefree time for William although often, watching Jayne enjoying herself at a party or function, he wondered why then, more than ever, she seemed almost glad to be without children; why, he wondered, hadn't she got pregnant again?

Having children was not something they'd discussed — William thought they rarely discussed anything important — but he had assumed that despite the miscarriage they would eventually have children. He assumed that Jayne felt the same.

When at last they did discuss it — on the long drive to Auckland in the middle of August that year — he learned from Jayne, surprisingly, for the first time, that she had been told after the miscarriage, and again since, that she'd probably, almost certainly, never be able to have children.

'Do you mind, Billy?' she asked. 'Really?'

'Not really,' lied William. 'But you should have told me before now.'

'I know,' she said. 'I am sorry.'

William thought she didn't sound sorry.

'It's not something I long for or anything,' he said. 'I just think it'd be nice for us, that's all.'

'It *would* be nice,' said Jayne although William sensed again that she didn't mean it.

Chapter 20

When, after a tedious and tiring five-hour drive, William and Jayne arrived in Auckland, William turned into Brockley Street, off Mount Eden Road, and stopped the car. He got out and stood on the street to take a long look at Brockley Cottage, standing so tall and broad and stately, in its park-like grounds, in front of the great bulk of Maungawhau, looking haughtily down the street.

There, he thought but didn't say, is where I grew up, where I lived for so long, where my darling Barbara still lives and is no doubt inside now, with my dear mother and aunt, waiting for our arrival.

He saw only the home to which he and Barbara, after school, would race each other, laughingly, up the gravel drive, knowing their mothers would be waiting in the parlour with a glass of milk each — cold in the summer, warm in the winter — and a plate of biscuits, cake, fresh scones or pikelets, or hot crumpets dripping with melting butter and golden syrup.

But Jayne saw it plainly, unfiltered by sentiment or nostalgia.

'Is that it?' she said loudly, sneeringly, as he got back into the car. 'The precious Brockley Cottage you're always talking about? Where you had such a *wonderful* childhood? That's really *it?*'

William heard the scorn in her voice and was taken aback. He tried then to see Brockley Cottage, at the end of the street, through his wife's cynical eyes but couldn't. So he simply said, quietly: 'Yep. That's it.'

'Billy,' said Jayne 'It's a bloody dump. A bloody old dump.'

The shared birthday dinner — so eagerly anticipated by both Barbara and William — had been prepared by the twins who had forbidden any contribution from Barbara, the joint guest of honour. It was a well-intentioned and carefully-planned affair, beautifully catered, but it was not a success.

Barbara sensed its pending failure as she, Tricky, William and Jayne stood together in the gloomy drawing room, surrounded by the Victorian furnishings once chosen by her great-grandfather, sipping their pre-dinner sherries and trying desperately to make small talk. At that point, even before they moved to the dining room, Barbara regretted the whole shared-birthday plan and wished only — but vainly — that she and William could have met together somehow, somewhere, just the two of them. Then, somewhere, they might have reminisced openly about the past and hinted — at least *she* would have hinted — at the affection they once and surely still felt for each other.

She knew, without doubt — it wasn't hard to tell — that as much as she now tried to be friendly to Jayne, William's wife simply didn't like her. She said all the things a host normally says to a guest whom she doesn't know well: 'How was the journey?' 'I like your car,' 'What do you do again, for a job I mean?' 'William says you have a lovely new house. That must be nice.'

Jayne's replies were perfunctory; she showed no interest in promoting any conversation. And when she did speak she referred to William as Billy which Barbara didn't like. She wanted to say: His name's William, always has been and always will be, but she didn't.

She didn't know why Jayne didn't like her but guessed it was some form of jealousy, and somewhere in her otherwise kind mind she was glad: she *wanted* Jayne to be jealous.

She also guessed that Jayne didn't like the twin mothers either. She didn't know why that should be; she loved her mother and aunt, as William did, and simply couldn't imagine why *anyone* wouldn't find them interesting; perhaps a little eccentric but interesting, lively and fascinating, all the same. In fact they were somewhat famous in Auckland. But then, she thought, Jayne knows nothing of Auckland.

She also knew — it also wasn't hard to see — that Jayne did not like Brockley Cottage. Even as she tried to make small talk, as they stood together awkwardly in the old room, on a huge, thick but ancient and somewhat dusty Turkish rug, adjacent to the French doors, she could see Jayne looking around, with barely-concealed contempt, at the bulky furniture, the heavy drapes and curtains, the ancient family portraits in heavy wooden frames, the mounted heads of two antlered stags jutting staringly into the room, the picture rail, the dusty bric-a-brac it carried, and the antique hand-printed floral wallpaper above it.

And earlier in the day, having escorted William and Jayne up the grand staircase, to William's old bedroom, she overheard Jayne say to William, with no attempt at wife-to-husband confidentiality, that the place was as much a dump inside as out.

'How can you ever want to come back here?' she heard Jayne ask William as she left them in the bedroom. 'It's like a spooky old haunted house or something.'

It was a comment which both annoyed and delighted Barbara. It annoyed her to have a virtual stranger insult the lovely old house which had been her home for most of her life, and the home of her family since her immigrant great grandparents built it, on their new farm, in eighteen seventy-two. But it *delighted* her to hear that William must have at least once expressed a desire to one day live there again.

Of William, she thought he looked mostly uncomfortable, perhaps embarrassed by Jayne's ill-mannered behaviour. She longed to be alone with him, at least for a while, and to speak of things only he and she understood and could share, but he seemed to be purposely avoiding her. Then, before dinner, she could see he was deeply engaged in conversation with Tricky. Perhaps, she thought, it was William's way of avoiding conversation with her although she hoped he really did like Tricky. She remembered that they got on well at the wedding although that was a few years ago.

As for Tricky, he seemed to be enjoying William's conversation as they shared their interest and experiences in the printing trade, in Auckland and New Plymouth.

The tension in the shadowy drawing room was dragged, by the four young people, reluctantly, heavily, like a dead weight, across the faded carpets and rugs, into the brightly lit dining room.

That room was rarely used by the three residents. It was a huge space with a high ceiling from the centre of which hung an elaborate, antique and somewhat dusty electric chandelier over a long, massive, heavily-legged and equally aged dining table with matching chairs covered in faded and threadbare brocade. A bold and elaborately carved dresser stood proudly against the wall, adjacent to the kitchen, from which liveried servants had once served the Brockley family then present with meat, poultry, fruit and vegetables from their own farm.

Heavily draped French doors looked out — like those of the parlour and drawing room — across the veranda into the dark of the north lawn and garden.

The twins, who had prepared and then served the elaborate dinner — Tricky volunteered to pour the wine — were proud of their work, proud of their adult children, and unreasonably excited by the whole occasion. As a result they were oblivious to the contrary mood, brought from the drawing room to the table, and so they gaily kept up a non-stop patter of chat which completely dominated the gathering.

Finally, once the twins had cleared and returned to the table, their prattling chatter turned to Barbara and William as children together. Much to the cousins' embarrassment their mothers laughingly listed their odd childish habits and idiosyncrasies, including their childhood dependence on each other's company and how they sometimes used to spend nights sleeping together.

How cute it was, said the mothers, that Barbara and William would pretend to be married.

Barbara found their revelations excruciating. She could see that the others — Jayne and Tricky but William too — thought the subject was not only inappropriate but was also being carried on too long. Evidently, once started on their reminiscing — speaking more to each other than the guests — the twins didn't want to stop. Barbara tried to interrupt, frequently, hoping to steer them into new subject territory, but she was always dismissed by her mother or aunt who insisted that Jayne and Tricky really *were* interested.

They weren't.

The final embarrassment came when the twins each began describing their experiences of childbirth thirty years since: how Mildred's labour was so easy, how Barbara's delivery was quick, and how loving and wonderful was her darling father, whom Barbara only vaguely remembered before he went away to be killed so tragically at the end of the war.

Millicent then described her much more difficult delivery of William, in gruesome and tasteless detail, until — prompted by a sudden thought — she stopped unexpectedly, her glass of wine held in mid-air.

'Oh, William, my darling boy,' she said, suddenly deflated. 'I almost forgot.'

Her changed tone left the others — including her sister — perplexed, looking at her, waiting anxiously for what was to come.

'What?' asked William, taken aback by his mother's sudden change of mood.

Millicent put down her wine and said bluntly: 'Your father died.'

William was astonished by news of his father coming so suddenly and inappropriately, on his thirtieth birthday party, from his slightly inebriated mother.

'What?'

Barbara and her mother were as surprised as William.

'You didn't tell me, Millicent,' said Mildred in a loud and angry whisper.

Millicent looked solemnly at nothing across the room and adopted a voice to match.

'I got a telegram from Australia—' she announced portentously before changing her tone '—from his bereaved wife, the bitch!'

'The bloody bigamist!' said a shocked Mildred.

'No, it's all right,' said Millicent slurringly into the air. 'We were divorced you know.'

'When?' asked Mildred indignantly. 'You didn't tell me.'

Millicent turned to look at her sister. 'I don't tell you everything, sister,' she said sharply.

'Well, I tell *you* everything.'

'Nineteen fifty-six. He did it in Australia. Got married again. Her name was Esme something and she sent me a telegram.'

'When, Millie? When did all this happen? How come I didn't know?'

'You didn't know because I didn't tell you.'

'So when did he die? What happened.'

'Just last year some time. Had a heart attack and died. Just like that.' She snapped her fingers then, and, as if coming out of a trance, she turned to William and said with contrition: 'I *am* sorry, William, darling. He was your father after all. I should have told you.'

'It's all right, Mother,' said William remembering only the beatings he received as a boy from his father's large, heavy and calloused hand. 'You told me now. That's the main thing.' He stood up and went around the table to stand behind her chair. He placed his hand gently on her shoulder. 'I think that's about it for tonight,' he said gently. 'Don't you?'

'But there's still the birthday cake,' insisted his mother who seemed recovered. 'And we have to sing Happy Birthday to you both, don't we?' she asked of Jayne and Tricky.

Barbara thought both guests looked rather uncomfortable.

'Are you sure, Mother?'

'Yes, Millie,' said Mildred. 'Are you all right?'

'Bugger it,' said Millicent firmly. 'I'm perfectly all right. What's all the fuss? Someone died? Now let's get on with it.'

"Getting on with it" involved Millicent, Mildred, Tricky and Jayne singing "Happy Birthday" to Barbara and William over the large and fancy cake which the twins had bought, at a discount, from the Farmers pastry kitchen, to which they had added thirty candles.

'Come on, you two,' said Jayne, when the singing was done. She sounded uncharacteristically bright. 'Make a wish.'

Given the way the evening had started and progressed, Barbara was relieved, as it was ending, that Jayne was doing her best to lighten the mood. However, feeling better about Jayne made her feel guilty about her secret wish. But she wished it anyway while also wishing she knew what William had wished. And she was thrilled that William had used his right arm around her waist to firmly draw and hold her close, their heads touching, so they could make their wishes and blow out the candles together.

Chapter 21

Back in New Plymouth William soon put away memories of the unhappy thirtieth birthday dinner at Brockley Cottage. At the end of that year — at just thirty years old — he received his promised promotion which meant moving off the factory floor into the production manager's office, moving out of overalls into comfortable town clothes, and moving from an hourly wage to a generous salary, an annual bonus, and the use of a company car.

He didn't even have to inherit his predecessor's car, which was given to the retiree as a parting gift, but was free to chose his own. He appreciated Jayne's opinion at that time and together they chose a new HR Holden sedan from Tasman Motors in Fitzroy. Jayne, meanwhile, had bought her own little Austin Mini which, William foolishly observed aloud, was the same as Barbara's.

William's increased income, and the freedom from obligatory overtime — often on Saturdays — meant he had more time for tennis and golf. And although he never bought a yacht he spent a lot of time sailing with friends and eventually joined them as a member of the New Plymouth Yacht Club which presented him — and Jayne — more opportunities to socialise and make more friends.

William had no trouble making friends.

Wherever he went he was liked, by old friends and new, young and old, and their wives. He was universally admired for his modest manner — despite his natural charm and good looks — his cool head, his kindness towards others especially the elderly and, more especially, lonely widows. He was considered remarkably wise for his age and whenever a controversial issue arose, at work, or in a club or organization, and whatever the level or extent of his involvement or responsibility, his advice was frequently sought and followed.

Meanwhile Jayne was happily swept along with William's professional and social advancement, learning quickly that although she rarely understood exactly what was happening, what was being discussed, and what the implications might be, her nodding smile, which passed for agreement and understanding, was interpreted as the unerring support of a beautiful, loyal and loving wife.

However most women — the girlfriends, wives, sisters and mothers of William's male friends and colleagues — while liking and admiring William, were not as enchanted as their menfolk by the young Mrs Conwyne. They thought that men — and their men in particular — were blinded by what they considered her overly made-up face, her expensive and frequent trips to the hairdresser and manicurist, her love of flashy jewellery, and her frequently-refreshed and expensive wardrobe, especially her predilection for mini-skirts.

William, though, was blithely, innocently, unaware of Jayne's reputation with women. Jayne, meanwhile, who had her suspicions based on the mostly veiled slights and rebuffs, chose to ignore them and instead enjoy the special places she went, the fine food and wine which was always there, and the important people she met, while at William's side.

William continued to improve his little house in Marfell. He enjoyed raising vegetables and flowers in his little greenhouse and setting them out in the gardens and beds he had planned himself. And where once his little parcel of land in Solebay Place was bare and unfenced, it was now bordered with fences and hedges, with a neatly laid path to the front door and a wide drive to a double garage at the side. The lawns, front, back and sides, were as level and smooth as the greens at the Dean Park bowling club.

And so the years in New Plymouth passed pleasantly for William while the grand affairs of the world, and of the rest of New Zealand, hardly touched him.

Jayne, though, was rarely content and easily disturbed. The introduction of decimal currency, in July nineteen sixty-seven, upset her considerably. Mr Currie sent his employees to a training course at his accounting firm but it didn't help Jayne who wished out loud — every night after work — that they could go back to the "old" money.

'It's so hard, Billy,' she said. "I *hate* it. I really do.'

The introduction of the new money didn't bother William. He didn't find it hard or complicated and wondered why it bothered Jayne so much. Nor was he directly touched by the other major reform of that year: the loosening of licensing laws which meant that pubs no longer had to close at six o'clock. His club memberships meant he could enjoy a social drink at any time but he was aware that it was a new freedom much appreciated by his staff, many of whom drank every night after work, at the old, famous and conveniently close White Hart.

Perhaps the biggest event of the time, which William knew would affect the New Plymouth and Taranaki economies for years to come, was New Zealand's first major oil strike which was made, in nineteen sixty-six, at the Maui I well off the Taranaki coast. Exploration for oil in the Maui II field began the following year.

The city was especially optimistic then and business boomed for Crosthwaite & Scott, William's employer.

Generally, then, William succeeded in making and enjoying a pleasant life for himself in New Plymouth. He and Jayne continued to make the most of their marriage as if to prove the doubters — especially Jayne's parents — wrong. Jayne had supported William during their early years, especially after the miscarriage, for which he was grateful. And then, as the years passed, she had remained young-looking and beautiful — he thought everyone agreed — loyal and faithful, at least as far as he knew. And if she sometimes spoke and acted as if she were still an excitable twenty-year-old bride it didn't seem to matter as no one else seemed to notice or mind.

Even during those easy-going years, while William was making the best of his marriage, Barbara was still always on his mind although he rarely thought of his mother. She, his mother, Millicent, wrote to him occasionally, and always sent him a special card on his birthday, but they rarely spoke on the phone. He knew more about her and his aunt Mildred from Barbara as he was free to make toll calls from his office as often as he liked. And so frequently — at least once or twice a week, sometimes more — he'd phone Barbara from work. Or she'd phone him. She, too, had her own office which meant they were able to speak often, as long as they liked, although not always as frankly as they wished they could.

All that happened, of course, without Jayne's knowledge. William knew that Jayne was unreasonably jealous of his past, of his strange childhood in a strange old house, and in particular what she considered his "weird and unnatural" relationship with his girl cousin, so he never told her about his conversations with Barbara nor of the Brockley Cottage news they contained.

Meanwhile, for Barbara, the unhappy and embarrassing events of the birthday dinner she shared with William, at Brockley Cottage in nineteen sixty-six, were difficult to forget. As well as remembering how her Aunt Millicent — unsober and rambling — had told William, and the room, that his father in Australia was dead, she recalled, especially, how Jayne had been such a disagreeable guest.

It wasn't that she personally cared about such things. Rather, she felt awful for William's sake; that he had to learn about his father in such a public way from his insensitive mother, and that he had to live every day with such a beautiful but plainly unpleasant wife. She thought he was being let down by the two women who should have supported him the most.

She wished *she* could have supported him more.

However, the lingering unhappiness of that difficult birthday night was overwhelmed five years later, in June, nineteen seventy-one, when, in the early hours of one stormy Sunday morning she had no choice but to telephone William.

Meanwhile, after ten years at Hervey-Harrison, Barbara was no longer considered a mere Girl Friday by Mr Blackie or anyone. She had learned much about the printing industry and had established herself as an important member of the management team.

Both Mr Blackie and his mother-in-law had so much respect for her, so valued her contribution to the firm's success, that they continued to reward her financially with regular salary increases and bonuses which, eventually, were converted into a profit-sharing plan designed to ensure her continued loyalty.

So generous were the firm's owners that she quickly accumulated what she considered a small fortune which she used to pay for essential repairs to Brockley Cottage, and to maintain the grounds, although the sheds and glasshouse were no longer used and had fallen into complete disrepair.

Of the Hervey-Harrison office and management team there when Barbara started only young Kay Coulson had left. She and her Ricky had married as planned in nineteen sixty-three. By the end of the next year she was heavily pregnant and while Barbara had always been kind to her, tolerant of her enduring adolescence, she was not sorry to see her go.

Better knowing by then exactly what the receptionist, telephonist and typist duties were, Barbara hired Helen O'Sullivan, a thirty-five-year-old local mother of two who was returning to the work-force having had a successful secretarial career in a large law firm. She was a couple of years older than Barbara, with the experience and maturity her predecessor had lacked.

Through her obvious hard work and willingness to learn, Barbara had also earned the respect of the office and factory staff. She managed to befriend the dour Salvationist estimator Derek Skinner and so discover that he was a secret "wizard" — Mr Blackie's name for him — with numbers and money. By winning his confidence Barbara was able to introduce many of his clever innovations in purchasing and stock control, machinery maintenance, accounting and investing, even staff and union relations, which all served to reduce overheads while increasing both productivity and profit. As a result Hervey-Harrison was able to pay better wages than its competitors which meant staff morale was high and union relations, via the Hervey-Harrison chapel — the printers' union — were especially cordial.

By then, Mrs Harrison's health was not good. She was still mentally alert but her body was failing. In the middle of July, nineteen seventy, she agreed with her daughter and Mr Blackie that she should move to a care home in Epsom, of which she, through the Harrison Family Trust, was a part owner. She received good care there without worrying about the family home in Victoria Avenue, which sold quickly, while still being able to attend the weekly meetings with Mr Blackie and Barbara.

Tricky, too, was still as much a friend as a colleague. He still lived at home in Waterview with his widowed mother whom Barbara had come to know well.

The twins thought it odd that Barbara's best and apparently only friend was a handsome and charming young man in whom she had no romantic interest or involvement and who, in turn, showed no interest in her beyond friendship.

'Such a dishy chap to have such a strange name,' observed Mildred more than once. 'Isn't he embarrassed to be called Tricky?'

Barbara could never explain Tricky to her mother and aunt. Nor could she admit to them that she had saved herself — continued to save herself — for William.

Although she hadn't seen William since their fateful thirtieth birthday dinner, she spoke to him often on the phone. She would have preferred to have seen him regularly, to talk more than they could or did on the phone, but, despite the affection she inferred from their sometimes-long telephone talks, their conversations never touched emotional subjects. Nor did William ever invite her or the twins to New Plymouth or suggest another trip to Auckland. He admitted once, by way of a round-about apology that, after the disastrous thirtieth birthday visit in nineteen sixty-six, Jayne had no interest in taking another trip to Auckland.

When William was next *compelled* to visit Auckland, in nineteen seventy-one, Jayne — angry and resentful — refused to go with him.

It was an ugly and unhappy time for everyone.

Chapter 22

Despite trying to never upset his jealous and sometimes moody wife, William sensed, at the beginning of nineteen seventy-one, that Jayne was becoming restless, acting irritably and unreasonably. When he asked about her unhappy mood she said she was bored; tired of living in their silly little house; that she didn't like Marfell; wished they lived closer to town, her parents and her job.

Wanting to please her, hoping to restore her formerly cheerful and easy-going disposition, William reluctantly sold the Marfell house and bought an unnecessarily large house, chosen by Jayne, in Fillis Street, opposite Pukekura Park. She had preferred a much more expensive house in Courtenay Street, near her parents, but William's willingness to move to town was not unconditional.

Jayne's desire for a new home was founded on an embarrassment which she knew was unfair and which she successfully concealed from William.

She was embarrassed by what she saw as their neighbours' apparent poverty. Of course they, her neighbours, were not poor, but in the nine years Jayne had spent in Solebay Place the lifestyle gap between the childless and career-minded her and her busy motherly neighbours had so widened it seemed unbridgeable.

She had her work at Currie's, which she considered glamorous and enviable, her trips to Wellington and Auckland seminars, regular hairdressing and manicure appointments, her own car, a fashionable wardrobe, and, thanks to William, regular socializing with the city's influential political and business leaders.

She knew that none of her neighbours had any idea of what she considered her busy and exciting life just as she had no concept of, or interest in, what she considered their narrow, boring and utterly unappealing lives. And, anyway, even if the gap between her life and theirs had been bridgeable, Jayne had no desire to bridge it.

William's willingness to move was also founded on embarrassment. But in his case he was embarrassed not *by* his neighbours but *for* them. Personally, he was quietly proud of what he had achieved since moving to New Plymouth. But he was aware that he had improved his little subdivision house as much as he could; to do anything more would border on ostentation, evidently flaunting his relative wealth.

William liked his neighbours and had no need or desire to impress them. If anything, he *envied* them. He envied them for their happy marriages, for the friendships they shared without having to leave the little Solebay Place community, and, above all — although he never mentioned it to Jayne and found it hard to admit even to himself — he envied them for the children they had, and might have.

In the end it was the fear that his apparent wealth and continued good fortune would embarrass his friends and neighbours, who were lucky enough to have children and be happy with their marriages, homes and lives in Marfell, that led him to reluctantly lead Jayne out of the modest little sub-division house he had bought in nineteen sixty-two, out of Solebay Place where he had always been content, to Jayne's choice of a big house in town, in Fillis Street, in which, as it turned out, he was doomed to unhappiness.

Having completed the move to Fillis Street Jayne suddenly announced, one weekend at the end of March, that she had quit her job at Curries where she had worked since leaving school.

'Fourteen years in the same job, Billy,' she said. 'I was only sixteen when I started that job. And old man Currie only hired me for my looks. Dirty old man.'

William knew Noel Currie. He was, indeed, an *old* man by then but William knew he had never been anything but a good citizen, a respected professional businessman, a responsible employer, and an honest, decent and loyal husband and father.

All the same, despite Jayne's unpleasant insinuation, he didn't think it unreasonable that she should be bored with her job after fourteen years.

'So what are you going to do?' he asked.

'Got a job at Farmers,' said Jayne.

The Farmers was the Farmers Co-op in Devon Street, New Plymouth's largest department store, just a few doors up the road from Currie's. It was owned by the farmers of Taranaki as a cooperative, unrelated to the Farmers department store in Auckland where the twin mothers still worked and where William had served his apprenticeship.

'Really?' said William. He was surprized. When, he wondered, had she arranged that?

'Yep. Start Monday week. Head of the whole beauty and make-up department. In charge of buying, displays, advertising, promotions, everything. Three girls. And a big fat pay rise.'

'What did Noel Currie say?' asked William.

'He never seem bothered,' said Jayne 'Said there's lots of girls want my job.'

'And how did you get the Farmers job?'

'The Max Factor rep recommended me to the big boss,' said Jayne. 'Got an interview with him and Bob's your uncle.'

It was a mystery to William. Although he vaguely knew the Farmers general manager he had no idea who Jayne referred to as "the Max Factor rep".

All at once, then, at the beginning of nineteen seventy-one, William felt he was losing control of his tranquil and predictable life. He was living in a new house — which was far too big for two people — in an unfamiliar neighbourhood, which he had bought reluctantly, only to keep Jayne happy. Meanwhile Jayne was evidently *unhappy*, despite her new address, and was moving to a new job thanks to a mysterious Max Factor salesman who, it seemed to William, had some sort of hold over her.

And then, suddenly, just after midnight one Sunday morning in the middle of June, he was woken by the phone jangling loudly, alarmingly, through the quiet house.

'First thing in the morning, I have to go,' he said to a sleepy Jayne who was more annoyed at being woken by the phone than sympathetic to her shocked husband. 'They need me there.'

He was sitting on the edge of the bed in his pyjamas, shivering only partly from the cold, his mind racing.

Above all his thoughts were with Barbara. She was evidently so distressed that Tricky Tremaine had taken the phone from her to give him the awful news.

And, aside from the terrible, unbelievable news, William didn't like hearing Tricky calling Barbara Barbs. He wanted to interrupt him, to tell him that her name was Barbara, not Barbs. And, anyway, he thought, what was Tricky Tremaine doing at Brockley Cottage so late on a Saturday night? Had Barbara called for his help? Or was he staying the night?

He didn't know and hadn't asked. He knew only what Tricky had told him, and while it was a lot, it was not enough.

He had to go. To be there.

'Well I'm not going,' said Jayne sleepily but defiant. 'And that's that.'

'I didn't think you would,' said William resentfully.

'I'm sorry,' said Jayne, who didn't sound sorry, and wasn't. 'I've got a big week ahead. Can't afford to be in Auckland.'

William was glad to be going alone. He wasted no time. He got dressed then, packed a bag, had a quick snack, and was on the road before dawn hoping to arrive at Brockley Cottage for breakfast.

Chapter 23

'I have to ring William,' said Barbara to Tricky when everyone had gone. 'He should know. Right now.'

'Are you sure?' asked Tricky. 'It's pretty late. It'll be morning soon.'

It was late because until then there had been no time. But at last, when the ambulance men had gone, having said there was nothing they could do, and the doctor had come and gone, having completed and signed the forms which the law required, she knew what she had to do.

Tricky was there, in constant support, for which Barbara was grateful as her almost hysterical mother had retreated upstairs and locked herself in her room.

'He should know now,' insisted Barbara angrily. 'For God's sake it's his own mother we're talking about.'

Tricky was more worried about Barbara's state of mind than William's need for sleep. He could hear shock, panic, fear and more in her angry and shaking voice. He wanted to say something sympathetic, something to calm her, but in the face of her anger and misery the words didn't come and so he said nothing. Instead, he steadied her as she walked up the hall, through the arch, to the phone in the cold lobby. He stood at her side as she dialled the operator and placed the New Plymouth call.

Barbara hoped, as she waited, that William and not Jayne would answer the phone.

Tricky held her free hand as she stood in Brockley Cottage's wide, spacious but gloomy and chilly entrance lobby. The veranda lights were still on and their outside glow passed through the old front door's coloured leadlight to cast shimmering soft-edged shapes of red, amber, green and blue onto the marble floor in front of the worried pair. Barbara had the phone in her right hand, to her right ear. Waiting for the connection, she could hear the wind rattling the door and the rain drumming tinnily on the veranda roof.

Then, suddenly, she turned to Tricky and said, nervously: 'It's ringing.'

Her eyes were red and wet, her cheeks were damp and blotchy, and she couldn't help sniffing.

'Hello?' It was William. He sounded sleepy. But thank God, she thought, William. Not Jayne

'Oh, William darling,' she burst out, not meaning to be loud, and not meaning to say "darling", but she couldn't help either.

'Oh, William,' she said again. She was sniffing lightly. 'It's so awful. I don't know what to say. How are you?' she asked foolishly before adding: 'Oh, how can I tell you?'

'Barbara. I'm here,' said a confused William. 'What on earth's the matter? Please.'

Barbara began sobbing uncontrollably. 'Oh, I can't,' she said, only half into the phone. 'I just can't.'

She collapsed against the wall, crying properly, while limply surrendering the phone to Tricky.

'William, it's Trevor Tremaine here, Barbs' friend from work.'

'I know who you are, mate,' said William. 'But what the hell's going on?'

'I'm so sorry, my friend,' said Tricky, 'but the thing is — there's no easy way to say it — your mother passed away tonight. Suddenly. Just a couple of hours ago. Barbs wanted to tell you herself but she can't. Can't do it.'

Barbara, leaning against the wall, weak in the legs, a little dizzy, thinking she might collapse, listening to Tricky talking to William about the awful events of the night, couldn't help feeling somewhat guilty that she secretly cared less about her poor aunt, dying so quickly yet with horrid pain, or her poor mother, suddenly separated from her inseparable twin, than about the pain William must be feeling at that moment, so far away in New Plymouth where she could do nothing to comfort him.

As she recovered, as Tricky was bringing the conversation to a close, she realized that William was *all* she cared about. She wanted to talk to him then but it was too late; Tricky was saying his good-byes.

'How was he?' she asked anxiously, standing up straight, wiping her cheeks softly with the flat of her fingers, almost fully recovered.

'He was mostly worried about *you*,' said Tricky. 'I said I'd look after you.'

'Oh my God, dear Trevor,' said Barbara. 'Whatever would I do without you?'

'He said he'll be here in the morning,' said Tricky. 'Early. As soon as he can he'll be here.'

That caused Barbara to burst into tears again. She fell then into Tricky's open arms where she felt safe not only from the horrors of the evening but also from the world, from nature itself, the unfair, unkind and unbendable rules of nature which took her aunt's life, and of society which, she knew, cruelly ruled poor Tricky's life just as they had kept her and William apart.

When she recovered she leaned back with a sigh and looked up at Tricky — who continued to hold her but loosely — and said what she'd never said and planned to never say to anyone, ever. But she said it anyway.

'The truth is, dear Trevor, that my cousin William — on the phone just now, in faraway New Plymouth — is the only man I've ever loved,' she said as her redded eyes overflowed with salty stinging wetness again. 'I love him with all my heart, I really do, I always have, but,' she continued, sniffing and trying to be brave, 'it's absolutely *impossible*.'

'I know,' said Tricky kindly. 'I really *do* know you know.'

'I know,' said Barbara trying desperately to return the kindness, sympathy and understanding she had just received from her special friend who had his own secret reason to be sad and lonely.

The storm of the night had passed by the time William arrived at Brockley Cottage that Sunday morning, after a fast non-stop journey from New Plymouth. Barbara, unable to sleep, made an early simple breakfast for herself and her mother, which her mother, alone in her room, didn't eat. During the making and eating of breakfast, the cleaning up after it, and the tense hour or more which followed it, Barbara was nervously alert for the distinctive sound of tyres on the gravel drive. As well as William she was expecting the funeral director, whom Tricky had arranged before he had reluctantly left well after midnight. She hoped William would arrive before the funeral director as she assumed he would want to see his mother before she was taken away.

It was getting light when she heard a car on the drive, stopping, its engine dying and a car door being quietly clicked shut. She dashed to the front door knowing the driver – whether it was William or the funeral director – must be properly greeted and let in immediately.

And so her heart raced in her breast, which felt hollow and empty, and she wanted to cry – she did cry – when she saw, in the grey morning light, that it was William, fast-walking from the car carrying a small bag. William alone. No Jayne.

And she gasped, and raised her flat and praying hands to her mouth, when William, seeing her shape standing at the open door, the yellow lights of the hall and veranda spilling around her, throwing confusing shadows onto the rickety veranda, dropped his bag and leaped up the equally rickety wooden steps.

He took her into his open arms.

'Oh, my darling Wiliam,' said Barbara, holding her beloved cousin as tightly close as he was holding her, 'I'm just so, so sorry.'

William said nothing at first. He just held her close; not moving; not speaking. Barbara felt wonderful but confused, her head turned and pressed against his chest, feeling the warmth of his body. She wondered how she felt free to call William "darling", and to luxuriate in his embrace, free of guilt and her usual inhibition, only because her aunt, her mother's twin sister, William's mother, had died so tragically and whose cold and lifeless body was still lying on he couch where Tricky had laid her and where she spent the last few minutes of her life in agonising pain. The thought made her feel horribly guilty so she wriggled away. William let her go; she guessed he may have been similarly confused for the same reason.

'Where is she?' William asked as he released Barbara and stepped back slightly.

Barbara, wishing only that she were still in his arms but knowing it wasn't possible, that William must have much more on his mind than hugging her, literally shook herself in order to assume a non-affectionate, detached persona.

'She's lying on the dining room couch,' she said. 'Trevor laid her there last night. After it happened.'

She saw William wince slightly at the sound of Tricky's name and so wished she hadn't mentioned him but she couldn't help it. He was there. He had done so much.

'The ambulance men didn't move her,' she said. 'There was nothing they could do. So she's still there. Just as she was. Except Trevor had to close her eyes when it was over. Oh, William, it was so awful. She was just staring up at the ceiling. Staring with bulging eyes.'

She lost her composure then and, crying again, turned to William who took her in his arms again but this time more, she sensed, from obligation.

'Oh, William,' she cried. 'It was *horrible.*'

William gently pushed her away then.

'But what actually happened?' he asked. 'Tricky didn't explain anything properly.'

Barbara stepped into the house then, ready to take William to his mother, ready to tell him everything, but he interrupted her.

'Hang on,' he said, 'I've got to get my bag.'

Once inside William dropped his bag at the bottom of the grand staircase knowing he'd be sleeping upstairs in his old bedroom, and was soon standing in the dining room with Barbara looking down on his mother's lifeless body. He hardly recognized her. She was lying on her back, on the couch, with her arms crossed over her breast. Her hair looked as stiff and dry as straw and her face was an eerie grey, stressed and taut; she seemed to be grimacing, her mouth open as if in pain. As a result her nose looked more pointed than he remembered. He saw her shoes on the floor and noticed that her tights were loose and wrinkled around her ankles; he thought it was a strange thing to notice.

'She looks *awful*,' he said quietly.

Barbara said nothing.

He leaned down and kissed his mother's forehead and quickly jerked back, horrified.

'She's so *cold*,' he said.

Barbara took his arm. 'She's dead, William,' she said. 'She's really dead.'

Chapter 24

'So what actually happened?' William asked. 'And where's Aunt Mildred?'

'Mummy won't come down from her room,' said Barbara. And then, pulling gently on William's arm, she said: 'Let's go into the parlour. The fires on in there. That's where it happened anyway. I'll tell you all about it.'

Once sitting — not at ease, but leaning forward towards each other on their great-grandfather's ancient but comfortable fireside armchairs — Barbara set out to explain the awful event which had brought her cousin hurrying back to Brockley Cottage. They were in front of the busy fire which Barbara had kept alive all night as if in memory of her late aunt who had, only a few hours since, enjoyed the warmth of its lively flames.

She explained that lately the twins had broken their habit of going to the Crystal Palace on Saturday nights in favour of staying home and playing cards with the radio on. She said they liked the old music on 1ZB.

'Trevor and I used to go out too on Saturday nights,' said Barbara. 'Sometimes, not always,' she added quickly, remembering William's antipathy towards her friend. 'But, anyway, a few weeks ago Mummy asked me if we would stop home and play cards with them. Five Hundred, see. They needed a foursome.

'Anyway, that's the thing,' she continued. 'We were playing cards when it happened.'

'But *what* happened?' asked a frustrated William.

'A brain aneurism, William,' she said looking directly at William while starting to weep a little. 'We didn't know it then but that's what the ambulance man thought and what the doctor was pretty sure about last night. She had a brain aneurism and died. A couple of minutes. Just like that. Oh, William, it was so awful.'

She wiped her eyes, with her flattened fingers, and then found a handkerchief from somewhere which she used to squeeze her nose. She felt tired and awful and suddenly realised what she must have looked like to William.

William, though, felt nothing but love and pity for his dear cousin who looked so stressed, so unhappy, and yet, he thought, so lovely. But he still wanted — needed — to know more about his mother's death. And so a tearful, sniffing, Barbara went on to explain that they were playing Five Hundred — 'We were starting our third game,' she said 'and Auntie Millie had called Misère' — when she, Millicent, had suddenly dropped her cards, almost threw them down, jerked her hands up to each side of her head, pressing her temples, and cried out.

'What did she cry out?' asked William anxiously. 'What did she say?'

'Oh, William, it was like a horrible scream. She sounded so frightened. I'll never forget.'

'Barbara, listen to me. Please,' begged William. 'What did she say? What happened?'

Barbara stopped crying then. She looked across into the flames of the fire and spoke to the glowing and pulsing embers of the fire rather than to William.

'She just said, cried out, so loud, holding her head, "Oh, Millie, I've got such a dreadful pain in my head". She sounded so frightened.'

Barbara turned away from the fire to look directly at William again.

'She looked so awful,' she said. 'Then, for what seemed ages, she just stared at Mummy opposite her at the table over there.' Without looking, Barbara indicated to the green-baize-covered card table behind them upon which lay the cards — including the late Millicent's hand of Misère — where they had been left. 'Her eyes were wide open and staring really weirdly.'

'Then what?' asked William.

'She tried to stand up,' said Barbara, 'holding her head. But she collapsed. Straight away. Knocked over the chair.'

Barbara stood up, turned and pointed to the place on the floor where her aunt had collapsed.

'That's when Trevor picked her up, carried her through into the dining room and laid her on the couch.'

William stood up then, too. Stood beside his cousin and looked blankly at the card table and the colourful round-cornered cards, stiff and shiny, scattered across its soft surface.

'Couldn't you do anything?' asked William.

'Dear William,' said Barbara gently, thinking it would be all right to link arms with him. 'She died in there, on the couch, where you saw her, where Trevor laid her. She took a big breath while staring up at the ceiling. Her eyes bulging. She looked so frightened. Then she breathed out and that was that. She really was dead. I've never seen it before but it was obvious. You could just tell. Trevor had to close her open staring frightened eyes.

'The ambulance came quickly but they said there was nothing they could do.'

She let go of William's arm and turned to look up at his face. She couldn't imagine how he felt. 'You all right?' she asked.

William looked down at her. She was surprised to see that his eyes were dry.

'Poor mother,' he said, slowly shaking his head in despair. 'What a way to go.'

Barbara could only nod in agreement.

'But what about Aunt Millie? William asked suddenly. 'Is she all right?'

'She's a wreck,' said Barbara. 'A complete wreck. Won't come downstairs. Nothing.'

'Oh, dear,' said William.

'Let me make you some breakfast,' said Barbara quickly. 'You must be hungry after that long drive.'

'And poor you,' added William, 'having to go through all that.'

Barbara shrugged. 'We have to wait for the funeral director,' she said.

William didn't seem to hear her. 'There's something else,' he said.

'What else?' asked Barbara, puzzled.

'It's weird, really,' said William.

'What?'

'Uncle Charles died,' said William.

It took Barbara a moment to remember who Uncle Charles was.

'Oh,' she said at last, not really interested. 'When?'

'In April,' said William. 'I went to the funeral. In Hamilton.'

'What's weird about it?' asked Barbara.

'Well, Mother and him, and Aunt Mildred,' said William. 'They never got on did they. They never reconciled. And now it's too late. He's dead and Mother's dead. And she never knew.'

'Nor Mummy,' said Barbara.

'And I didn't know till the funeral,' he continued, 'that Aunt Ruby had died already. Nobody even told me. Cedric should have told me.'

Like her mother and aunt, Barbara had never been interested in the twins' older brother and his family so she didn't quite understand William's distress.

'They were so good to me,' said William sadly. 'You would have liked them, you know. And they would have loved you too. And now they're gone. Like Mother.'

After his mother's small funeral William returned to New Plymouth. Barbara continued to treasure the memory of his presence — sleeping in his old bedroom, next to hers — for the four days, seven hours and thirty five minutes he spent in Auckland, mostly at Brockley Cottage, mostly with her, arranging his mother's funeral, attending his mother's funeral, and tidying up his mother's simple affairs afterwards.

There was a small life insurance policy, the proceeds of which, together with a small savings account, went to William. Brockley Cottage had been left to the twins — their older brother Charles Brockley, who might have expected to inherit it, was dead and had never wanted it anyway — and so William's mother's share was predictably left to her sister or, if Mildred died before her, or at the same time, the house would be passed to Barbara and William jointly.

'Your mother's will will be the same,' said William to Barbara as he prepared to leave for New Plymouth.

They were standing together at Brockley Cottage's back door, in the cool shadow of Maungawhau, beside the ramshackle stables.

'So one day all this will be ours?' asked Barbara, seeking confirmation of her own understanding and spreading her arms to symbolically embrace the entire freehold estate: three acres of almost priceless Mount Eden land, and the two-storied mansion, built in eighteen seventy-two and incongruously called a "cottage" by the cousins' rich and reportedly ruthless great-grandfather, Ebenezer Partington Brockley, one of the so-called Fathers of Auckland.

'Unfortunately, yes,' said William tactlessly.

Barbara was hurt by William's offhand remark.

'What do you mean, *unfortunately*?' she asked. 'I *love* Brockley Cottage. I always have. Don't you?'

'It doesn't matter,' said William who didn't want to debate the subject.

'It *does* matter,' said Barbara indignantly. 'It matters to me. I'll live here till I die. And I won't change a thing about it.'

William said nothing to that. Instead he kissed Barbara lightly on the forehead, turned, stepped carefully down the few steps to the path and strode away to his car parked beside hers in the old stables.

He waved to Barbara before he got in the car, and tooted his horn as he turned into the drive. And that was the last Barbara saw of him, her dear cousin, until nineteen seventy-six when they shared an expensive dinner to celebrate the auspicious birthday when, as the saying goes, life begins.

Chapter 25

When Barbara returned to work after her aunt's death and William's short visit, after only a week away from her office, she was surprised at how she had been missed; how her return was so welcome; how, apparently, she was so highly respected. In particular, she was surprised by how many decisions, on matters both trivial and crucial, had been deferred by others until her return.

She realized then that in the ten years since she started at Hervey-Harrison, as a Girl Friday, she had learned a lot about the printing industry as well as about the management of people and money. She knew that the departmental managers and their staff, as well as the firm's customers and suppliers, saw her, and treated her, as a putative general manager.

She wasn't that — at least not officially — but nor was she a Girl Friday. What she had become was an efficient manager, relieving Mr Blackie of many of his duties and instructing departmental managers about theirs.

She was also in receipt of a recently increased and especially generous salary reflecting the company's faith in her while cultivating her loyalty. It meant she could easily afford the help she needed to care for her increasingly frail and demented mother.

Mildred Conwyne survived her twin sister by five unhappy years.

She never returned to her Farmers cafeteria job; she didn't resign but simply stopped at home, leaving her bedroom only to put something into her body or let something out.

A week after the funeral her manager telephoned to check on her welfare but Mildred had decided to never again answer or speak on the phone. A week later he wrote a letter to which Barbara replied explaining that in view of her mother's sudden mental and physical decline the Farmers were free to remove Mildred Conwyne from their payroll, without obligation, just as they must surely have already removed her late sister Millicent.

Mildred's agonising grief for her departed twin — a loss that was, she said, as painful as having her arm brutally ripped away from her body — expressed itself permanently on her face, in her deportment and attitude. Although she was only fifty-nine years old she looked and acted like a stooped and frail old lady. She chose only drab and unflattering clothes; she stopped getting her hair done and stopped using make-up. The beauty and vivacity she once shared with her sister simply evaporated. Indeed, even if they might be captured and returned — and Barbara so wished they would — she would have declined to accept them, so deep and permanent were her loneliness and melancholy.

Barbara was personally aware of how awful it must have been for her mother to lose her twin. She could only imagine what her own life would be like without William.

Eventually, five years after the loss of her sister, by which time she often forgot Barbara's name or, sometimes, didn't even recognize her, Mildred had a mild stroke which meant she could no longer be cared for at home. Barbara, whose responsibilities at Hervey-Harrison continued to increase, placed her mother in a nearby care home where, helpless and bewildered, she died only a month later — at the end of October, nineteen seventy-six — from a second but overwhelming stroke.

Despite speaking to Barbara at least once a week, William had somehow failed to tell her — in June when it happened — that Jayne had left him for Merv, the mysterious Max Factor salesman whom he had never met. He finally told her at their shared fortieth birthday dinner in Auckland although he didn't provide any details then — it had taken him by surprise only a few weeks since — and was glad she hadn't sought any.

The separation happened quickly and painlessly on the Saturday of Queen's Birthday weekend. William had come home from golf to find a short note from Jayne, printed in black crayon, in large girlish letters, on a large sheet of paper unmissably anchored to the fridge door, telling him that she had taken all her things and that she was moving to Wellington to live with Merv and that she was sorry and he could get rid of all the clothes and shoes and old make-up she'd left behind because she didn't want them any more and that it wasn't his fault and she was sorry but she loved Merv it was real and that was that.

William never heard from Jayne again. She never contacted him nor sought anything from him including money or a divorce. Before long it was as if she had never existed.

Barbara always kept William informed about her mother's failing health which had been a convenient excuse to speak to him regularly. However, the sad old lady was still alive in August when William came to Auckland for their fortieth birthday dinner.

'Jayne won't be coming,' he said without explanation.

'Well Mummy won't be up to anything of course,' Barbara said. 'And I won't ask Trevor, so there'll just be the two of us.'

Barbara had chosen Antoine's, a cosy and romantic restaurant in Parnell where and when, alone, they spoke a bit more freely than they had for years. It was then, over dinner, that William confirmed what Barbara had guessed about Jayne. He didn't volunteer any details then, and, as he was obviously hurt and confused, Barbara didn't press him. But it did give her the excuse to reach across the table to sympathetically cover his hand with hers. And while she sincerely felt sorry for him she couldn't help secretly, but guiltily, rejoicing.

Later, at home, before they went to bed, they merely hugged goodnight at Barbara's bedroom door. Barbara was disappointed. Although the hug may have been a bit closer than was seemly for a *happily* married man, Barbara wondered why the newly-free

William hadn't at least kissed her goodnight. Surely, she thought, he must have wanted more than a hug. Surely he wasn't being faithful to his unfaithful Jayne. And then, the next morning, when William left for New Plymouth, she was disappointed again when he said goodbye with another kiss-free embrace.

Two months later, when she told William that her mother had at last succumbed to her unconsolable grief, Barbara again secretly but guiltily rejoiced that she might once again have another legitimate reason to share a loving embrace — or perhaps, this time, more — with the only man she had ever loved.

'You *will* come to the funeral, won't you?'

'Of course I will,' said William. 'I'll see you soon.'

By the time of his Aunt Mildred's death — meaning another trip to Auckland for the funeral and, hopefully, another dinner with Barbara — William had been on his own for four months. In that time he had repaired relations with Jayne's father who still lived in Courtenay Street — Mrs Galvin was dead by then — who admitted that his younger daughter had always been a "silly young thing".

He had always been friends with his sister-in-law, Lois McCoombs and her dour but honest and decent farmer husband, Mick, who said they didn't blame him for anything and thought that Jayne was stupid and was probably having a mid-life crisis although she was only thirty-five.

His many friends at his clubs were supportive although William noticed they were careful about what they said about Jayne. He knew that most of them had had known her and her family longer than he, and guessed they too may have thought, like her father, that she was indeed a "silly young thing".

His colleagues — and especially his managers — were equally supportive and equally discreet about Jayne. William knew that while they hardly knew her socially they would have known her family and, perhaps, her dubious reputation.

Now, having accepted his new situation, and despite the sadness of the occasion — his aunt's funeral — William was glad to have a reason to visit Auckland. He longed to hold Barbara in his arms again, free of guilty thoughts about his estranged wife. He also thought Barbara deserved a fuller explanation of his past and present circumstances than he felt able to provide in August.

'While you're here I think we should have another nice dinner,' said Barbara. 'Do you think I'm awful?' she asked. 'Straight after the funeral I mean?'

William smiled. It was exactly what he'd hoped for.

'To be honest, I think you must be a bit relieved that she's gone,' he said.

'I am,' said Barbara, pleased that William understood.

She knew he would.

Chapter 26

'Brockley Cottage should have been Uncle Charles's if he'd lived,' said Barbara. 'Not ours.'

They were at dinner that night, after the funeral.

'Except he never wanted anything to do with it,' said William. 'He told me himself in no uncertain terms.'

'I wonder why?'

'He wouldn't say,' replied William. 'Wouldn't even talk about it.'

'Well it's ours now,' said Barbara. 'Or soon will be.'

'And what the hell are we going to do with it?'

'We'll keep it, won't we?'

William grimaced.

'What?' Barbara was again shocked by William's attitude to Brockley Cottage. 'It's where I live, William,' she said. 'I've got nothing else. At least you've got a nice home in New Plymouth.'

William grimaced again at the mention of Jayne's characterless house waiting emptily for him in New Plymouth. It didn't feel at all like home. But Barbara didn't know that. Not then.

He could also see that she didn't understand his attitude to Brockley Cottage. *He* couldn't understand her impractical loyalty to what he considered nothing but a huge financial liability. The old building was in desperate need of repair while the inside was no better than a dusty old furniture museum. And while he understood the twins' loyalty to the place, and their refusal to make any changes, he couldn't understand why Barbara wanted to keep living there now that their mothers were gone.

150

'Well?' insisted Barbara.

'Nothing, really,' said William not wanting to again hurt Barbara's feelings on the subject. 'But, listen,' he said, hoping to lighten the mood without necessarily changing the subject, 'I was talking to a man at the funeral. A neighbour he said but I didn't know him or remember him.'

'Brockley Street's changed a lot,' said Barbara. 'All the old people, well, they're all gone aren't they.'

'Well this bloke, he wasn't old,' continued William. 'He said all the local kids say Brockley Cottage — they don't call it that; they just call it the "Big House" — they say the Big House is haunted. They say that two witches live there, one old and one young, and that kids dare each other to run up the long drive, onto the veranda, and bang on the door with the knocker and run away.'

'That explains a lot,' said Barbara with laugh.

'But it really *is* run down,' said William. 'It really is. You must admit. And so much land.'

'I do my best,' said Barbara who continued to be hurt by William's criticisms.

'Let's forget about that for now,' said William quickly. 'We'll figure it out later.'

Hurting Barbara was the last thing William wanted. He wanted to change the subject. He reminded her that he'd been a virtual bachelor since June and told her about the note on the fridge.

Barbara was relieved to move on from the subject of old Brockley Cottage and glad to sense that William was ready to talk about Jayne and their separation. And so she asked him: 'What's this Merv like, then?'

'No idea,' said William. 'Never met him.'

'He must be *amazing* if she left you for him,' said Barbara who unashamedly held William's hand again across Antoine's white and starched linen tablecloth.

'I s'pose so,' said William.

'So Mummy and Auntie Millie were right all along,' said Barbara when William told her — confirmed — that Jayne *was* pregnant on her wedding day.

'Not only that but I think they were right about the entrapment thing,' said William.

'You mean...'

'I read about it,' interrupted William. 'Since, I mean. Huge mixed-up psychological stuff. Complicated.'

'But what happened? A miscarriage, right?' said Barbara. 'Mummy and Auntie Millie guessed that too.'

'On the honeymoon,' said William who reacted to the horrid honeymoon memory by pulling away his hand from Barbara's and leaning back in his chair.

'Oh, William,' said Barbara with all the sympathy she could muster. 'How awful. For you both.'

'There's more,' said William.

'What more?'

William leaned forward again, retook Barbara's hand, and looked directly, intently, into her enquiring eyes.

'She didn't even *want* children.'

'What?'

'Well, after a few years I actually thought it would be nice to have a couple of kids,' said William relaxing again, leaning back in his chair. 'Can you understand that? Even with Jayne?'

'Of course I can,' insisted Barbara.

'And then I found her pills,' said William. 'I didn't even know what they were.'

'She was on the *pill?*' Barbara was astonished.

William nodded.

'After the miscarriage she said the doctors told her she could never have children. Physically impossible.'

'But she was on the *pill?*' said Barbara. 'All that time?"

'All that time,' confirmed William. 'She worked in a chemist, for God's sake. Knew local doctors. Knew about those sort of things. Lois, her sister, told me later that Jayne was one of the first women in Taranaki to be prescribed the pill.'

'So she was lying about not being able to have children?'

'Lying,' said William. 'All that time lying.'

The next day William reluctantly returned to New Plymouth annoyed with himself that he hadn't said — couldn't bring himself to say — at their dinner, or later at home, or even as they said goodbye on the Brockley Cottage veranda, what he so wanted to say merely because, well, he didn't know why.

Why am I so confused? he thought as he drove. Jayne? Aunt Mildred's death and funeral? The wonderful dinner and talk with Barbara? The thought of inheriting Brockley Cottage together? The state of the old place? He didn't know but decided again that he would — must, soon — tell Barbara exactly how he felt and take it from there.

Meanwhile, knowing that not only was William's marriage over but also that it was never planned and never happy anyway, changed everything for Barbara. And yet, when William was gone, she was annoyed with herself — angry, even — that she hadn't told him how she felt, how she had always felt, when she had the chance, after the funeral, at dinner, or later, or any time before he left.

But, she told herself, there will be another chance. And next time I'll take it. I'll definitely take it.

Chapter 27

After a short but decent interval, Barbara returned to work much to the surprise of her colleagues and employees. They expected her to be distraught at the death of her mother, reluctant or unable to return to work so soon. For the sake of propriety she pretended to be more bereft than she felt. But how, she wondered, could she explain to those who don't know, that some deaths bring more relief than grief to the living?

It was only when she caught up with Mr Blackie that she learned that during her short absence his dear Down Syndrome daughter Mary-Jane had died suddenly. She felt sadder about that — sad for the poor young woman but especially sad for Mr Blackie and his wife — than she did about her own mother. She knew she should feel sadder than she did — that others probably would — but in fact she felt glad. Glad for her sad, sick and demented mother, who never recovered from the sudden and shocking loss of her twin sister. Glad for William who, she now knew, was happily free of his unhappy marriage. And glad for herself that she had been constant to the promise she made to never marry any man if she couldn't marry William.

Imagine, she thought with horror, if I were married now just when William is not. What a dreadful irony that would be.

She had no idea when she might see William again. They'd made no arrangements about anything including what they might do together about Brockley Cottage. In fact, she had no idea at all of what the future might hold. She knew only that she now lived alone in Brockley Cottage which she jointly owned with William, and that while she loved the old place, where she had lived for most of her life, William, well, she didn't know exactly what William thought of the place but she knew he didn't cherish it as she did.

So, what next? she wondered.

What happened next was a surprise — or, rather, a series of connected surprises — of such import that they permanently, dramatically, changed the course of her life.

And William's.

It began at morning tea, on her first day back at work. Mr Blackie came into her office, apologized for interrupting her, and told her about his Mary-Jane. He asked how she was, if everything was all right. Barbara knew he was referring to her own bereavement. She assured him she was fine.

He then asked if he could sit down and, once sitting, made a surprising announcement in his plain no-nonsense manner which Barbara had learned to appreciate.

He said that while she'd been away, he and Mrs Harrison, his mother-in-law, had agreed to ask her to join the board of directors.

'There's only the two of us at the minute,' he said, 'plus Arthur of course—' Barbara dealt almost daily with Arthur Knight, the firm's accountant, and knew him well '—and we think you'd be a welcome addition. We meet properly once a month and we'd welcome your opinions and contributions.'

That was it. A huge surprise. Something Barbara had never expected.

'So, young lady,' said Mr Blackie, 'what do you think?'

Barbara hardly had time to think and so, almost *without* thinking, hardly believing what she'd heard, said, asked: 'Really?'

'Yes, Barbara,' said Mr Blackie who rarely called her by her Christian name; rarely called her by any name. 'Really.'

'Well,' said Barbara whose racing mind — the very mind which Mr Blackie and Mrs Harrison had come to admire — had done its thinking, 'yes, Mr Blackie. Absolutely yes. And thank you. And Mrs

Harrison, too. Thank you both. I can't believe it. But, yes. Thank you.'

Then, another surprise, Mr Blackie said that while things were being sorted out she should immediately arrange to give herself a generous salary increase. Barbara hid her shock but could barely believe the large amount mentioned. It made her think she'd been underpaid for years.

'The firm is very profitable now, as you know,' continued Mr Blackie, 'due in large part to you, so—' another surprise '—you'll also be entitled to a share of the profits. Arthur is drawing up a plan now.'

There was more by way of businesslike conversation, Barbara's questions and Mr Blackie's answers about routine matters including where and when the board met and details of the duties and responsibilities of a director of a private firm such as Hervey-Harrison.

Finally Mr Blackie brought the discussion to a close with an apparent aside, speaking as if it were something he'd just remembered, although Barbara could see he was a little embarrassed.

'I must say, Barbara,' he said, trying hard to sound informal, relaxed, 'you were sorely missed while you were away, after your mother and all that.

'Mrs Harrison made the point,' he continued, still looking somewhat awkward, 'that with your mother gone, you looked after her for so long didn't you, selflessly, but now you're completely on your own. There's no "Mr Right" looking after you is there. You're what Mrs Harrison calls a career woman. You know what I mean I hope.'

Barbara knew what the poor embarrassed man meant. He meant that he and his dear old nice-but-clever-and-cunning mother-in-law — who knew nothing of William nor anything of Barbara's personal circumstances — were now confident that at her age, single, with no man in the picture, childless, with no other responsibilities, a house to maintain — although they didn't know quite how big a house it was — and the prospect of enduring spinsterhood, she would undoubtedly have to keep working at least until retirement. Therefore, went their obvious reasoning, given her experience and proven value to the firm, she should be induced to keep working at Hervey-Harrison as long as possible.

'I know what you mean,' she said kindly.

The man who had employed her as a Girl Friday in nineteen sixty-one looked relieved. He was standing at her door now, fifteen years later, having said his piece, ready to leave.

'You've done well, Miss Conwyne,' he said with a smile. 'We really appreciate it. And don't forget,' he added with a wagging finger, 'your new salary starts today. And, by the way,' he said over his shoulder, 'while you're at it, get yourself a new car.'

She did. She bought a sporty new blue Ford Escort from John W. Andrew in Khyber Pass.

'Congratulations,' said William on the phone when she told him about her dramatically changed status at Hervey-Harrison. 'You deserve it. I'm very proud of you.'

While she loved to receive William's compliments they weren't enough. There was so much she wanted to discuss with him including, to start with, Mr Blackie's bald assumption that she was a confirmed spinster. But William was in New Plymouth which made even a gentle hug of affection and approval impossible let alone the detailed discussions which she now considered urgent.

They were urgent because her suddenly changed situation came with implications which would profoundly affect her future.

But she couldn't imagine *any* future without William.

Now, at forty, she knew that believing and fearing what she had read in her great grand-father's *Chalmers's Own Modern Family Health (Anatomy, Surgery & Medicine)* book she found in the Brockley Cottage library, she had inadvertently, unnecessarily, sent William away to another city, another job, another family, an entirely new and different way of life, and ultimately into an unhappy and childless marriage to an unfaithful wife.

Twenty years ago. Twenty wasted years. Twenty years wasted.

But what of the next twenty years? Or more? A career woman? An unmarried career woman? A spinster?

They say life begins at forty, she thought. Might life be about to begin for me and William? Together? She knew she was now committed to Hervey-Harrison for twenty years or more; a commitment that would likely bring more financial rewards and security than she had ever dreamed of.

But what would that mean to a woman alone?

And what of William? What of *his* future? He once reluctantly made a commitment to a marriage that didn't last. Would he be ready, at forty, to make another commitment? Because William too had wasted twenty years. He didn't even have the benefit of the child who, boy or girl, would have been about fifteen years old and to whom he would surely have been a wonderful father.

And I'd have been a wonderful aunt, she thought.

As William was free — if not actually divorced — and her own future at Hervey-Harrison secure, Barbara felt able to abandon the pretence of respect for William's marriage which she had maintained for almost fifteen years. She knew that neither of them could afford to waste another twenty years apart. She also knew, with absolute certainty, that she wanted to spend the rest of her life with William and, with equal certainty, that he would want to spend the rest of his life with her.

But how and when, she wondered, could she make that happen?

Chapter 28

When William returned to New Plymouth, after his aunt's funeral, he felt he was in a foreign country. Driving down Leach Street, and then up the Gover Street hill, he felt lost. Suddenly the familiar looked foreign. He stopped on the street, across the road from the Fillis Street house which, after five years, he still thought of as Jayne's house. He stepped out of the car, studied the house as if for the first time, and decided it was modernly angular and ugly, devoid of charm.

Inside, it didn't feel like home. Despite being small compared with the two-storied vastness of Brockley Cottage it was large compared with his simple but familiar Solebay Place home. Big and eerily empty and echoey, sinister and unwelcoming, he couldn't help comparing its stark architectural modernity, and Jayne's modern furniture, with the grand and aged graciousness of Brockley Cottage, and the comforting if cluttered cosiness of its familiar rooms.

Later, unpacked and fed, he sat outside for the rest of the afternoon and into the cool evening, enjoying his melancholy aloneness. It was there, that night, on the deck, where, for five years, he and Jayne had entertained his friends, and Jayne's family, with lively barbecue parties beside the pool and under myriad coloured lights, he decided he no longer had any desire or need for any human company or friendship but Barbara's.

In Auckland, after their Antoine's dinner, and despite Barbara having to deal with her mother's death and funeral, he had come close to properly confessing his undying love. But for some reason he hadn't. Alone on the deck that night he was therefore full of regrets. And so, before he was overcome with tiredness, born mostly of sadness and depression, he decided he could not live another year, let alone another twenty, without telling Barbara what he truly felt, and had felt — secretly, painfully and without respite — for twenty years.

Whatever the consequences, he decided to sell Jayne's house, cut his ties in New Plymouth, and return to Auckland where he would find work and, if Barbara agreed, live with her at Brockley Cottage. They did, after all, share ownership of the old place. And even if it was a bit of a wreck it was at least their shared wreck. Now, he hoped, they could make it their shared home.

He wanted to tell her when she gave him her Hervey-Harrison news, on the phone, at the end of November, but, cautiously, decided to wait until the house had sold and he had thought through all the details and implications.

Jayne's house — such a fine property, said the agent, a highly desirable address — sold easily and quickly over the holidays.

At the beginning of January William did the decent thing by the people he had come to know and like in New Plymouth although he sometimes did it more from courtesy than desire. He farewelled his cousin Cedric, who was largely responsible for introducing him to New Plymouth society, including the extroverted, notorious but thoroughly likeable Lois McCoombs.

Lois, in turn, insisted on a personal meeting in town. They met in the same coffee shop where, at the beginning of nineteen sixty-one, William had first met Jayne. There, fifteen years later, Lois apologized again for Jayne and her behaviour, for introducing him to Jayne in the first place, and for her late father's occasional boorishness.

She eventually said goodbye on the street with a tearful hug.

His various club goodbyes were painfully drawn out — and somewhat incomplete as many people were still on holiday — and although he liked the individual friends he had made at each club he didn't like the corporate fuss caused by his resignations and farewells.

His resignation from Crosthwaite & Scott in the middle of the month, when the factory reopened after the holidays, was the hardest. His departure, at the end of January, was accepted with genuine regret by Mr Scott, the firm's managing director. William and he had become good friends — they frequently played golf together — and it was Giles, as he insisted William should call him, who had quickly recognized William's ability as a manager of people and so promoted him to the senior position of general manager which he held at the time of his resignation.

His final day with the firm — a Friday — was marked with a low-key gathering in the lunchroom at which Mr Scott made a small speech and presented William with an especially bound and engraved copy of a valuable book, recently produced by the company: a facsimile of *The history of Taranaki : a standard work on the history of the province*, which was originally published in New Plymouth in eighteen seventy-eight.

After that, there was no turning back. And if William felt even a hint of regret it was promptly dismissed by the thought of Barbara waiting for him at Brockley Cottage which was once again to be his home.

He had turned in his car by then and replaced it with a new Cortina from Phillipps Motors. The next morning, his new car packed with not much more than his clothes, he set off for Auckland. At forty years old, when life is said to begin, he was returning to old Brockley Cottage where he hoped he and Barbara would pick up where they foolishly and mistakenly left off when he left for New Plymouth in March, nineteen fifty-eight.

Curiously, within a month of her mother's death, Barbara received another stunning surprise which she happily told William about when he arrived.

She didn't notice it at first but in the second month realized that the unwelcome visitor who had come and gone, with more or less inconvenience, and more or less regularity, for nearly thirty years, had not returned and never would.

The irony, which she saw but William didn't, was that it was that visitor's first unexpected arrival in nineteen forty-eight, when she and William were just twelve years old, which brought about her anxiety about cousins having children. And it was that same event which so frightened William who, knowing nothing of such things, believed he had somehow wounded his cousin, making her bleed profusely, as together they had embraced, closely but innocently, in their half-sleep.

Before William arrived Barbara bought a new double bed; a luxurious new Sleepyhead with a deep box-spring base and the most expensive ticking available. She installed it in the master bedroom, upstairs at the north end of the house, and, for a few dollars, persuaded the Farmers' burly delivery men, who had already hauled it up the grand staircase, to push her great-grandfather's ancient four-poster bed against the inside wall, behind the door.

William was, of course, more experienced in the one important thing in which Barbara was not experienced at all. But his love for her, and the twenty years he spent longing for her — for her company if nothing else — made him especially tender. He could never forget how painful it was, at just twenty years old, to be in her presence, to be near her, to be living with her in the same house, sleeping in the bedroom next to hers, to watch her going out and having fun with other young men, while he pretended he didn't care.

Twenty years later, including fourteen years of marriage — for better or worse but mostly for worse — he was happy not only for himself but also for Barbara who, as she explained it, was forever free of the worry which had kept them apart for so long.

And so, at forty years old, after twenty years apart, Barbara and William Conwyne were free at last to express their love without limit or inhibition.

PART TWO

Chapter 29

Once together at Brockley Cottage William and Barbara didn't marry. They saw no need. But as their Brockley Street neighbours moved on or passed away, to be replaced in time, one at a time, by others who knew nothing of the past but lingering rumours and traditions, they were soon assumed to be, and referred to as, Mr and Mrs Conwyne, the rich, eccentric and reclusive owners and occupiers of the historic "Brockley House" which was named — according to common understanding — after Brockley Street.

Married or not, unconcerned with what their neighbours and others might think, William and Barbara, together at last, were completely at peace with the world.

But the lives of people who know nothing but tranquillity and contentment — hardly aware of any other state or of other people — are so empty of interest that nothing can be written of them better than "they lived happily ever after". Indeed, so quickly did William and Barbara establish and maintain their pleasant routine that only sweeping generalizations can be made of the age they spent happily in each other's company as husband and wife.

At last, though, after the passing of a decade of precious years, fate intervened to bring — to Barbara especially — worry and stress, fear and uncertainty, sufficient to make the William and Barbara Conwyne story interesting again.

And so, to resume.

At first William had tried but couldn't get a job in Auckland similar to the one he had left in New Plymouth. He found his Conwyne name was a distinct disadvantage; that Barbara had acquired a reputation in the printing world as a tough competitor, and it seemed — William had to surmise what he wasn't told — that potential employers who otherwise valued his experience, and liked him personally, did not approve of his relationship to Barbara Conwyne whom they universally but incorrectly believed to be the managing director of Hervey-Harrison.

Looking for work is not a full-time job no matter how many applications are made and interviews attended. As a result, in the beginning, William had many free hours alone at Brockley Cottage; sometimes, many consecutive days.

To fill time he began to tidy the grounds.

One of his first and most poignant chores was to demolish the tree hut which was old even when he and Barbara had played in it as children. The huge old monkey apple tree had grown and stretched since the hut was built by his grandfather in the nineteen twenties — for his twin daughters — so distorting the hut's architecture of wood which had anyway become dangerously rotten.

He made a bonfire of that rotten wood onto which he threw the equally rotten wood of the swings built at the same time by the same man for the same twin daughters, and on which the young William and Barbara had played happily, for hours, so many years ago.

As he worked, not unaffected by childhood memories, he began to seriously survey the state of Brockley Cottage, its outbuildings and gardens. He'd always known that the old property — left in the hands of the unworldly twin mothers by their wastrel father, and then to Barbara alone, with no knowing male attention — was in considerable disrepair. But now, spending twenty-four hours of most days in and around the house, he suddenly discovered the truly alarming condition of the place which he and Barbara now owned.

He began compiling a schedule of maintenance chores listed from the most urgent — and that alone was a lengthy register — to the cosmetic. In the weekday hours between Barbara's leaving for and returning from work, except the time he took to do the household shopping and prepare their evening meal, and even on the weekends, William began, slowly at first but with increasing urgency and enthusiasm, to address the property's essential repairs. And where the work was beyond his ability — due to the effort required or his lacking the essential tradesman's skills and tools — he drew on his own funds to pay for the required material or labour.

Before long — perhaps six months into the year — William stopped looking for paid employment believing that restoring the valuable and historic Brockley Cottage property — the house, the outbuildings, the grounds and gardens — was more important, and certainly more rewarding, financially and emotionally, than working in town at a routine job for mere wages. He also knew that Barbara's Hervey-Harrison income dwarfed anything he could earn in a printing factory.

So gradual was William's eight-year restoration of Brockley Cottage, its grounds and outbuildings, including the converted stables in which were stored their cars, that by the time he was finished there were few neighbours who remembered the property's once shameful condition.

That, though, marked the end of William's period as a master renovator. But so thorough had he been, and so diligent in continuous maintenance of the house and freshly-landscaped grounds, that it would be more than twenty-five years before such a restoration was again required.

In the course of those eight years of constant work William had not only learned a lot but had also made many friends amongst the local corps of tradesmen who recognized both his aptitude for practical work and his genial personality. For work they considered too small — 'Not worth starting the truck,' they said — they recommended him as a home handyman for hire. Before long he had enough work to fill his day, meaning he often had to manage the supermarket shopping between jobs, dashing home at the end of the day to get the dinner ready for Barbara who usually came home physically tired and emotionally drained.

His support — always steadfast — became more important a few years later when Barbara's professional life was turned upside down by unpredictable and unpleasant events over which she had no control.

Meanwhile, once her new life with William had settled into a reliable routine — when William was running the house as well as his own little business — Barbara felt confident enough to begin gently but firmly assuming more responsibility at Hervey-Harrison. She wasn't driven by ambition but simply to fill the management vacuum left firstly by old Mrs Harrison who, at eighty-five, rarely left her care-home, and, secondly, by Mr Blackie's slow, reluctant but inevitable withdrawal from the firm's day-to-day affairs in preparation for his retirement.

Mr Blackie was a little over seventy-one in nineteen eighty-four when he finally retired although even then not because he wanted to but because his wife Heather, Mrs Harrison's daughter, had been stricken with Parkinson's disease. It was then that he and Mrs Harrison — after quietly congratulating each other for their foresight in securing Barbara's loyalty with a profit-sharing directorship — appointed her managing director in full charge of the entire Hervey-Harrison enterprise.

It was a remarkable appointment for a woman in the printing industry — or any industry — at that time. It was a challenge which Barbara was proud to accept and certain she could meet especially as her life at home with William was always there as a safe and unchallenging retreat.

A year later, when Derek Skinner — Barbara's strange, religious but inordinately clever estimator — retired, Barbara lost one of the last links with the old Hervey-Harrison management team. Only Tricky Tremaine, her friend and sales manager — by then he had two salesmen working for him — remained to remember her as

Mr Blackie's shy young Girl Friday of almost twenty-five years earlier.

Barbara was especially sad to see Derek go. It was she who had discovered his aptitude for applied mathematics. She used him to advise her on everything including capital expenditure on expensive new plant, and especially on investing the firm's short- and long-term surpluses; he even helped with union negotiations. In all, the humble Derek was willing, cooperative, happy to help Barbara in any way he could, while humbly having no desire to use his talents for personal gain.

While she granted Derek a generous retirement bonus, she otherwise respected his wishes and allowed him slip away, at the close of the business one Friday in September, nineteen eighty-five, without an official farewell. Other than knowing he was still a bachelor, and still an active member of the Salvation Army, she knew nothing of his private life.

She *did* know, however, that he would be impossible to replace. And so she hired *two* men in his place: one, an experienced middle-aged professional print estimator from Clark and Matheson, a rival firm, to do the largely clerical work of estimating, invoicing and bookkeeping, and an ambitious young chartered accountant to provide the professional advice and stewardship which the unqualified and unambitious Derek had formerly provided so willingly as part of his duties.

The ambitious young accountant, Geoffrey Redcar, came from a well-known and respected London accountancy firm. He admitted to Barbara that he might have expected a partnership there in due course but insisted that he wanted to "get into business".

'God, Mrs Conwyne,' he said at one of his interviews, 'I just *love* New Zealand, and I *love* business.'

Barbara was astonished. She'd never heard anyone, young or old, enthusiastically say any such thing about business.

'But *this* business?' she asked, thinking a medium-sized printing company in New Zealand would seem far from exciting or glamorous to an ambitious young Englishman late of The City.

'Hell, yes,' Geoffrey replied adamantly. 'Small privately-owned business. So much potential. The *future*. Can't wait.'

While Barbara thought his attitude was somewhat unhealthy for an otherwise well-adjusted young man about town, she also thought that he and his passion for business would be a financial asset to Hervey-Harrison.

Her instincts in this, as in so many of her business decisions, proved to be excellent although the unhappy cause in which he had to help her was not one she could have anticipated nor ever wanted.

Chapter 30

By the beginning of nineteen eighty-six, when Barbara was in her fiftieth year, she was innocently, naively, at ease with herself and her life. Her position, experience and authority at Hervey-Harrison were never questioned, she knew she had the loyalty of her staff and customers, and, thanks to her large salary and annual profit-sharing, she was financially secure, whatever happened, for the rest of her life.

Just as important — for her and for anyone successful in business — she had a happy and secure home life with a loving partner who supported her in everything she did professionally while providing the essential escape from the pressures of the working day.

And then suddenly, unexpectedly, tragically, the powers she thought were hers, to control her life and steer it into the future, were cruelly swept away in three fatal steps which left her utterly shocked and bewildered. Eventually, inevitably, and quickly, they changed the course of her life and, of course, William's life too.

The first shock came on her fiftieth birthday when she learned, on arriving at work that Monday morning, that Mr Blackie had died suddenly from a heart attack late in the afternoon of the previous day. Evidently he was doing the lawns and had come inside complaining of feeling unwell.

He was seventy-three years old with no history of heart disease, at least according to Mrs Blackie.

William had planned a special birthday dinner that night at Antoine's, their favourite restaurant, but Barbara was not in the mood. She was unnerved by Mr Blackie's death and said she had to prepare herself, emotionally, for the funeral where she was to speak. She knew she'd also have to deal with Mrs Blackie — Heather — who had never recovered from the death of her dear Mary-Jane ten years earlier and was herself dealing with her own debilitating Parkinson's disease as well as worrying about her frail and failing mother. Mrs Harrison, at ninety-four, was still mentally strong but too physically weak to attend her son-in-law's funeral.

The old lady's own death early the next year, nineteen eighty-seven, was followed almost immediately by that of her still-grieving daughter Heather, Mrs Blackie. They both died even before probate had been granted to Mr Blackie's estate; nothing had been settled. As the three deceased together owned all the Hervey-Harrison shares, and as each had left one third of their own shareholding to each of the other two, their other third to "Miss Barbara Conwyne, the firm's managing director", their almost simultaneous deaths created a tortuous and almost unheard of legal triple circularity which took more than a year for the lawyers and courts to resolve.

For the first but not last time Barbara was glad to have Geoffrey Redcar, her new accountant, at her side. Although he was not a lawyer he was more than capable of dealing with the many lawyers involved, regularly parsing the court's ponderous decision-making, reporting progress to Barbara, and, from the beginning, accurately predicting the inevitable outcome: that by the end of nineteen eighty-eight, Miss Barbara Mildred Conwyne of Brockley Cottage, Mount Eden — as she was referred to in court documents — would be deemed to have inherited the business, freehold land and buildings of Hervey-Harrison Limited, Commercial Printers of Burleigh Street, Mount Eden, Auckland.

Barbara was horrified.

'Oh my God, darling,' she said to William when she was eventually told of the court's decision, 'I don't want it.'

'But you *like* your job,' said William. 'You've always liked it.'

'As a job I like it,' she replied. 'But to own it, the whole place, lock stock and barrel as they say? All the staff. All the money. The building. The responsibilities. I don't want any of it.'

'I just don't *want* it,' she repeated to Geoffrey Redcar the next day. 'What on earth am I going to do?'

'It's Friday,' said her clever young accountant. 'Give me the weekend and we'll talk about it on Monday.

It was two years before Barbara completely overcame the horror that descended on her that day at the end of nineteen eighty-eight.

She couldn't blame Geoffrey Redcar for the awful years of working and waiting. On the contrary, he did something she could never have done: he used his international European and American contacts, made during his accounting career in London, to travel the world, starting in Australia, and to eventually secure an outright sale of the business to an Anglo-German publisher of medical, veterinary and other scientific literature. That company needed a secure, experienced and fully-equipped printer who, due to product content confidentiality, foreswore outsourcing, to print their publications in house — in English and French — and distribute them in New Zealand and Australia, the Pacific — including French Polynesia — and parts of English-speaking South-east Asia.

She also couldn't thank him enough for the price he got for the business although what seemed like an outrageously large sum to her was considered a bargain by the buyer who had no idea, thanks to Geoffrey Redcar, just how desperate was the seller.

Barbara didn't know how Redcar found his buyer, nor exactly what took place during the final negotiations, mostly in London and Melbourne, over almost three months. But during those two years, as the sole owner and managing director, she had to keep managing the whole business, including staff morale — with the help and support of both Geoffrey, when he was in town, and Tricky Tremaine, her reliable friend and sales manager.

At last, though, at the end of nineteen ninety, she received full payment for the business on the legal understanding that she would never again work in the printing industry, never approach any of Hervey-Harrison's clients for any reason, nor ever disclose its business affairs to any of its competitors or anyone.

The buyer installed its own management team. After a long two month's overlap, Barbara was gone.

Tricky Tremaine, her secretly troubled friend, whose mother had died in nineteen eighty-five, left Hervey-Harrison then. He planned to start a new life, working in real estate in the Bay of Plenty. Helen O'Sullivan, the receptionist, also left the firm. She had been loyal to Barbara during the two troubled years of Barbara's sole ownership and said she couldn't imagine working there for anyone else. She was near retirement age and said she and her husband, a retired police detective, planned to take a world trip.

When at last it was all over Barbara felt terrible. She admitted it to William. After enjoying her Hervey-Harrison job for so long, having learned so much, and being so grateful to Mr Blackie for employing her in the first place, and then to him and his mother-in-law for having so much faith in her potential and ability, she ended up wishing she had never heard of Hervey-Harrison and its well-meaning owners.

She retired to Brockley Cottage to manage her wealth and learn, from William's experience and example, to enjoy a less busy but more fruitful and satisfying life. She had no Hervey-Harrison friends. She wrote to Tricky Tremaine occasionally but there was now absolutely no one in her life but William.

With William's patient help she learned to live life at his calm and unhurried Brockley Cottage pace, and to slowly forget not the enjoyable years she spent at Hervey-Harrison but the last two years of unavoidable stress which began with three deaths and ended satisfactorily only as a result of Geoffrey Redcar's efforts on her behalf.

Once again the years passed quickly and peacefully as they do for people who have learned to balance productive activity with therapeutic leisure. And although they had worked independently for so long — William at home and in his own little business, Barbara immersed in the hands-on management of Hervey-Harrison — the old cousins soon and happily resumed the life they had left off as teenagers. They had plenty of money from the sale of Hervey-Harrison, more than they could ever use. William stopped playing tennis, or socializing with his tennis club friends, and gradually reduced his jobbing work until he was able to spend his entire day with Barbara working around their shared home and garden.

Barbara then realized that stopping home with William, day after day, rarely going out — alone or with William — was all she had ever wanted. After all they'd been through, together and then separately, since their shared childhood, she could barely imagine anything better. She was living in the only home she had ever known with the only man she had ever loved. It was, she realized, all she had ever wanted; her dreams had come true.

William had experienced more of life than Barbara. He had lived in another city, away from Brockley Cottage, in his own home, with a wife who was not Barbara. He had made many friends in New Plymouth, in clubs and societies, where he was always active and always welcome.

Although he was happy, and happy for Barbara — that she was free of her Hervey-Harrison obligations, happy to be home, happy that they could spend every minute of every day and night together, needing no one else, no other company — he was also aware that their lives were completely intertwined. He could see that they had become as interdependent on each other as their twin mothers had been, and that they probably appeared — and were — just as strange, eccentric and reclusive.

Yet while he was aware of how they must appear to others — an evidently rich old pair, getting on for sixty, who had no children, no friends, who rarely went out except once a week to do their shopping — he decided he didn't care. And as Barbara seemed oblivious to how they must look to outsiders, how their life together, and their relationship to each other, so resembled the strangeness of their mothers, he resolved to not mention it to her. That she was so obviously happy and content made him happy and content.

They treasured their new life together knowing that at the end of the day, literally, the other would be there to give the unquestioning and uncompromising love and support they had each always longed for.

That's all they had ever wanted and needed. And now, at last, they had it. Every day.

Chapter 31

However much anyone is jealous of their own happiness and contentment, their tranquillity is bound to be disturbed by life's unpleasant events, occurring without warning, utterly beyond their control; events which cannot be foreseen, denied or ignored.

Barbara, scarred by her unpleasant Hervey-Harrison experience, was always more worried than William that something would occur to spoil their comfortably pleasant lifestyle. And, of course, despite the cherishment of their shared home life at Brockley Cottage — enhanced by a lifetime of memories — her anxiety was naturally justified: the outside world *did* sometimes intrude. Not often but often enough to temporarily interrupt and annoyingly blight their peace.

Such is life.

But when, in the winter of two thousand and nine, William was diagnosed with cancer, the interruption to their contentment was sudden, utterly unexpected, and far from temporary.

William ascribed the back pain — an early but unrecognized symptom — to some heavy work he had been doing in the garden. He, and Barbara too, assumed it would abate if he avoided such work allowing his old body to repair itself as it usually did. But Barbara became worried when the pain remained, and the always active William complained of fatigue. Even when he forced himself to work he often ended the day unhungry for his usual hearty dinner. Then, suddenly, he noticed that his trousers were loose; he was losing weight, rapidly.

These sudden symptoms were a mystery to Barbara but not to the hospital specialist to whom they were urgently referred by their suspicious doctor. But even the specialist preferred to wait for scans and other tests — all a mystery to the medically naïve and always healthy William and Barbara — to confirm his diagnosis of advanced pancreatic cancer.

There were, of course, the usual platitudes and therapies. William found the chemical treatment to be especially debilitating while Barbara found it agonisingly painful to helplessly see his pain and distress.

'Oh, darling William, what on earth can I do?' she would ask every time she brought him home, exhausted, from the clinic.

'It's enough that you're here,' William always replied. 'We're together. That's all I've ever wanted. To be together.'

'Oh, me too, my darling,' said a frequently weeping Barbara. 'Me too.'

Before long William couldn't manage the grand staircase. Barbara bought a hospital bed which she installed at one end of the ballroom where he could look out through the lofty windows, across the veranda, to the north garden which, unfortunately, was becoming overgrown absent his constant grooming.

There, in that vast, empty, uncarpeted and echoing space, Barbara sat at William's bedside, sometimes for hours, until at last he fell asleep with the help of the strong drugs she helped him take.

After a few months they were told the disease appeared to be advancing, not retreating. William said the pain, too, was increasing, despite the hospital's best efforts and therapies which seemed to William and Barbara to be worse than the disease.

They had to take what was offered. There was no choice; no option. But even the oncologist assigned to William admitted, near the end of the second and evidently futile programme, that it didn't seem to be working, and in fact — he confessed — was rarely effective, but sometimes…

'You never know,' he said. 'It's worth a try. There are recorded cases…'

That was at the end of twenty-ten, just before Christmas.

It was then that William — seventy-four years old, thin, sallow and weak, and sick of repeated hospital stays and clinic visits which he found exhausting — decided to decline further therapy, as many sufferers do. He wanted to stay home to be cared for by Barbara, taking only the prescribed and effective painkillers.

It was a decision Barbara supported; she hated seeing William in as much pain from the so-called therapy as from the spreading disease.

Finally, though, on Easter Sunday, twenty-eleven, when hospital consultants and specialists were mostly on holiday, when hospital staffing levels were at a holiday low, as were hospital services including laboratories which were staffed to only emergency levels, when even William and Barbara's GP clinic was closed, William was struck with a crisis which caused him to scream from a pain beyond Barbara's ability to manage. A pain so severe it caused him, eventually — before Saint John's help arrived — to black out so completely that Barbara thought he was dead.

He wasn't dead but, for a time at least, he wished he were. In hospital again, perhaps for the last time, he received the pain relief that only a specialist doctor could prescribe and a specialist nurse could administer.

The next day the hospital grudgingly arranged for an ambulance to get William home.

'He'd really be better off in a hospice,' said the doctor. 'There's a place waiting for him now. At Saint Joseph's.'

'It's what he wants,' insisted Barbara firmly. 'To die at home.'

The doctor nodded; humanely understanding but professionally sceptical.

'You *do* realize it'll only be a few days,' said the doctor. 'A week at the most.'

'I know,' said Barbara. 'And so does he. Don't worry.'

The doctor looked searchingly into Barbara's eyes, saying nothing but concentrating hard, trying to enter her mind and read her thoughts. Eventually, seeing nothing but a blank return gaze, and so surrendering to her resolve, he turned down his mouth, shrugged slightly, and looked down to reluctantly sign the prescription.

'Will that be enough?' asked a worried Barbara as she took the small piece of paper. She couldn't imagine how either William or she could manage without the painkillers. 'So much pain?' she added.

'Plenty,' replied the doctor grimly. 'More than enough, really. Just in case, you know. As you say, it could get bad at home. No nurses or anything. You do understand, don't you?'

Barbara nodded. 'Yes. Thank you,' she said.

A hospice nurse was assigned to visit Brockley Cottage daily.

Barbara waited anxiously the next morning for the nurse's first visit; she wanted to ensure she was suitably professional, mature and sensible, fit for the duties and responsibilities which surely awaited her.

Her name was Beverly. She was sixtyish, overweight, wise, kind, experienced and sensible.

Barbara was glad.

Working slowly, speaking gently as she worked, she showed Barbara how to ensure William was comfortable, and how to help him take the pills.

'Tomorrow you can help me give him a wash,' she said when she was leaving. 'He'll like that.'

'Tomorrow?' asked Barbara.

'Yes,' said Beverly. 'Tomorrow. Every day. Until, you know…'

'What time?'

'Same as today,' said the nurse. "About nine.'

Her little white car was on the drive at the foot of the veranda steps.

'You're quite sure?' asked Barbara as she stood on the veranda to see the nurse out. She desperately needed the nurse's reassurance.

'Oh, yes, Mrs Conwyne,' said the nurse, standing at the open door of her car. 'Please don't worry. Every morning about nine.'

'Tomorrow then,' said Barbara. 'About nine.'

'Yes,' said Beverly. 'About nine.'

William slept heavily that day, on the edge of consciousness, the pain breaking through only occasionally. Late that fine and autumnly-cool April evening, Barbara sat at his bedside to wait with him as darkness slowly filled the ballroom.

'Won't be long now, darling,' she said, as she held the wet sponge to his dry and sucking mouth while she gently stroked his forehead.

William manged a weak almost indiscernible nod.

Once his thirst was quenched Barbara went quietly, on slippered feet, down the length of the darksome ballroom, down the long hall, through the arch and into the cold lobby where she unlocked the front door, leaving it slightly ajar. Returning to the ballroom she went to the massive fireplace and switched on the lamp which she had earlier placed on the mantlepiece. Against the marble base of the light she rested a stamped and sealed envelope addressed to Mr Trevor Tremaine in Tauranga.

Then, in the wide gilt-framed mirror, tilted down over the mantelpiece, she checked her not entirely grey hair before returning to William's bedside. She bent, then, and kissed his cold forehead which caused him to stir, open his eyes, and work them hard to focus on her face.

'It's time, my darling,' she said.

William nodded.

'Are you still sure?'

William attempted a smile and nodded weakly again.

'Here we go then,' said Barbara as she gently lifted his head from the pillow with her left hand while helping him, alternately, sip from a glass, a concoction she found in the Veterinary section of her great-grandfather's *Chalmers's Own Modern Recipes and Remedies for Home and Farm,* and take sufficient of the prescribed pills, one or two at a time, as well as some of those which he and she had saved or filched during his numerous hospital stays and clinic visits.

She lay his head back on the pillow, gently, and although he smiled crookedly up at her — the only woman he had ever loved — with gratitude and relief she could see almost nothing through her wetted eyes.

She saw enough, though, to take her share of the potion and pills, swallowing them with grim determination, before putting the empty glass and bottles on the mantelpiece, switching off the faint yellow light, kicking off her slippers, returning to William's bed, and lying down there beside the only man she had ever loved.

— THE END —